I0625868

THE MCDERMOTT FIFTY

BOB HERZBERG

WOLFPACK
PUBLISHING
— EST 2013 —

The McDermott Fifty

Paperback Edition
© Copyright 2020 Bob Herzberg

Wolfpack Publishing
6032 Wheat Penny Avenue
Las Vegas, NV 89122

wolfpackpublishing.com

Paperback ISBN 978-1-64119-785-4
eBook ISBN 978-1-62918-203-2

THE MCDERMOTT FIFTY

PROLOGUE

He had ridden his horse down the low hill near their property, expecting Emma Lou to come running out of the cabin with her arms held wide waiting to embrace him. He thought it was strange that she didn't appear, and when he spotted the cabin door swinging wide open in the harsh wind of a Nebraska winter, he got scared. Real scared.

He spurred his mount down the short trail and leapt off the saddle when he got to the front of the cabin. He let the reins trail along the ground and ran into the open doorway, not sure of what he'd find inside. He stopped immediately after clearing the doorway and his eyes searched the front room. A thick coating of snow had made its way into the room and covered the worn rug and old wooden chairs. He could tell that a fire had been going in the corner stove but had now been blown out long ago by the winds. A pot full of coffee was still on it. He went over to the stove and felt the pot. It was cold as ice.

He looked around anxiously, seeing no disturbance in the place outside of the neglect in leaving the door open to the elements.

His tall figure took huge strides over to the bedroom door and threw it open. He saw that the bed had been made and that the room seemed normal. He went over to the makeshift wooden closet and saw that Emma's clothes, what few there were, were still hanging there.

He moved quickly back through the front room and then left the cabin. His heart was racing in his chest as he jogged around the side of the house. It was then that he heard the creaking/banging noise coming from somewhere in the distance, and he ran towards the sound.

When he got to the backyard, he stopped suddenly and stared at the grove of trees some sixty feet back away, their branches bare and the leaves blowing violently along the ground in the mounting wind.

However, one particular tree wasn't bare.

His eyes welled up with tears as he stared at her. He didn't know when it happened, or how long ago, but it seemed that in all that time, no one had bothered to cut her down. The rope they had used was old, but still strong enough to keep her body dangling some ten feet off the ground in the dead of winter.

He went to his knees then, sobbing. With his head bent over, his wide-brimmed Stetson fell to the ground and, mixed with the pile of fallen leaves, started to blow away.

He was away too long, he told himself. He shouldn't have gone back to the army and left her out here all alone. He was convinced that things had gotten better; that they would finally leave them in peace. The local law had said it and the federal government had said it, and like the biggest fool in the world, he had believed them.

Absently, he reached out with a long arm and grabbed his Stetson before it flew up into the high mountain ranges and was lost forever. Purposefully, he put it back on and set it straight and firm on his head.

He vowed they would never take anything from him again...

CHAPTER ONE

WHEN CHES KINDERSTROM STEPPED OFF THE TRAIN, HE FELT HOT, dirty and too damn tired. The exceptionally warm spring didn't agree with him, but few things in life ever did, it seemed. He didn't like sleeping on trains and didn't like the folks around him who didn't let him sleep even when he tried to. They were either glad-handing salesmen who talked out of both sides of their mouths or sweaty cowboys passing through the cars loudly proclaiming their presence, as if their smell wasn't enough. Both groups seemed to be looking for a poker game; something that Kinderstrom thought was best left played in a saloon.

A tall, reedy man with short blond hair, his blue-grey suit seemed a bit large for his thin frame. As he looked down the platform, he took off his Stetson and mopped his forehead with a neatly folded monogrammed handkerchief. He gripped the handle of a once-clean suitcase he had bought in Stockholm, but the trip had worn it down somewhat. Seeing absolutely no one waiting on the platform, he hastily shoved his handkerchief in his pocket and pulled out his pocket watch. Snapping it open, he looked at the time and cursed.

It was 11:05 on a bright crisp Tuesday morning, that day in April of 1885.

Stationmaster E.E. Hinds had seen Kinderstrom standing alone and came out of his office.

He asked, "Everything all right, sir?"

"I'm waiting for my ride," Kinderstrom said tightly. He hated little old railroad employees as well. He hated their shuffling little walks and their colossally stupid questions. No, Kinderstrom just loved standing there on a train platform in the middle of goddamn nowhere at eleven in the morning for his health.

Hinds read the hostility in Kinderstrom's face and decided to leave.

"Excuse me," he said, barely touching the brim of his cap and walking away. Kinderstrom's narrowed eyes followed him as he made his way back to the station office and slamming the door after him.

These western trash, he thought. In Europe, they'd laugh at these rowdy vulgarians with their dirty clothes and their rough ways; pulling guns every time someone even looked at them wrong. He wouldn't even be here if not for McDermott. *This big deal of his had better be good!*

It was then that he heard the buckboard coming; unfortunately for him, the sound came from the other side of the railroad tracks. He looked across and saw a young man in range clothes driving a buckboard come into view. Kinderstrom saw the man's leather-gloved hands give a slight pull on the reins, bringing the buckboard to a halt. Then he saw the man scanning the area, looking back and forth and every which way until his eyes stopped on Kinderstrom's lone figure staring at him from across the tracks.

It wasn't certain whether the man took note of Kinderstrom's contemptuous glare when he finally spotted him. The thin man staring back at the cowboy just shook his head in disbelief.

Still seated on the buckboard, the man waved at him from across the tracks.

He shouted, "Mister Kinderson!"

Kinderstrom gritted his teeth and said irritably, "Kinder*strom*!"

The cowboy grinned stupidly and replied, "Oh. Sorry. Guess I'm on the wrong side of the tracks, ain't I?"

Kinderstrom couldn't believe his ears. Are they all this brainless out here?

The cowboy said, "Wasn't sure which side the platform was on, but don't you worry, Mister Kinderson, I'll turn Elvira right around the bend there and we'll be there in a hitch." Then he grinned again and said, "Hope the twelve o'clock to Denver doesn't show up early. I'd hate for Elvira and me to get flattened whilst crossin' this here set o' tracks. Mister McDermott wouldn't like that one bit."

But I would, Kinderstrom thought.

The man shook the reins and, with a shout, turned the buckboard in Kinderstrom's direction.

Kinderstrom had sat next to the man and didn't say a word. He sensed the cowboy's tension then. He already figured him to be a talkative fellow and that the enforced silence probably made him feel awkward.

That was his problem, Kinderstrom thought. I'm not here to entertain him with conversation; he's here to deliver me to the boss—and he couldn't even be on time to pick me up!

The cowboy cleared his throat and asked, "Uh, is anything the matter, Mister Kinderson?"

Kinderstrom replied curtly, "Yes, once again, and hopefully for the last time, my name is Kinder*strom!* Now I'll ask you a question, if you don't mind."

The cowboy grinned and shrugged his shoulders.

"Why, sure," he said, "ask me anything."

"Are they all as stupid as you back at the ranch?"

Kinderstrom saw the cowboy's shoulders tense up and his arms stiffen as he held the reins.

Then the man turned his head slowly around and said, "The last man that called me that is cold in the ground with a bullet in his noggin'." He paused as he glared at Kinderstrom, then he added, "If you weren't friends with Mister McDermott, I'd put one in you and dump you out here for the coyotes."

Kinderstrom returned the man's glare with his own and forced himself not to swallow nervously. He had dealt with highwaymen back in Europe and knew that to show fear was a mistake.

When he replied, he made sure there was sufficient arrogance in his voice. There was nothing so good as acting as if you're God's gift to mankind and the other guy's trash.

"But I *am* Mister McDermott's friend," he said with just the right touch of insolence. "And because of that, you're going to keep your stupid mouth shut and continue to take me to his ranch, is that clear?"

Kinderstrom saw the cowboy's veins knotting in his forehead and his lips quiver at the corners. He could see in the man's eyes that he wanted to tear him apart, but that some barely concealed sense of self-preservation was restraining him.

The cowboy didn't answer him. He just turned around and faced the trail again. There was nothing he could do to buck the boss and he knew it. Not now anyway...

When the buckboard pulled before the two-story frame house, Kinderstrom was surprised at its modesty. This was the home of Tad McDermott, a simple affair that housed the man who owned thousands of acres of prime land.

In their intercontinental communications, Kinderstrom noted that McDermott never once mentioned his wife, so he had no idea whether she was even still alive. He didn't think anything of this at first, since their letters were strictly about business; but now, as he entered the house and removed his now dust-covered hat, he wondered if he was going to be greeted by the man himself or his wife.

Kinderstrom noticed that the cowboy who brought him also removed his hat, showing a full head of dark brown hair, not very well combed. Looking through an archway, he saw the living room beyond. He noted the carpeted floor, the tastefully chosen upholstered furniture, and the lace curtains over the large windows. There was a fireplace with a mantle some thirty feet away on the other side of the room, and above it, a painting of a red-headed, bewhiskered Scotsman in kilts. Kinderstrom noted that the figure didn't have a set of bagpipes in his hands, which is what he, as someone who rarely associated with Scots, would expect them to carry. Instead, the Scot was holding a rather huge sword, and by the fearsome scowl on his ruddy face, he seemed to be ready to do battle.

Kinderstrom heard footsteps and he turned towards the carpeted stairway on his right. He saw a tall man in his forties descending and then stop a few steps from the bottom and stare at him. He was dressed in a neat brown suit and string tie; his crisp white shirt beneath the coat practically gleamed. His hair was starting to gray at the temples and a mustache covered a small, grim little mouth. It was Kinderstrom's guess that a smile did not come easy to this man.

"Mister Kinderstrom."

It wasn't a question or a greeting, it was a statement.

"My name's Len Cagle."

After introducing himself, he stood there and waited. It took an awkward second or two before Kinderstrom realized that Cagle expected him to walk over to the stairway and shake *his* hand; not the other way around.

Kinderstrom suppressed an exasperated sigh and walked over to the stairway, climbing the first couple steps and shaking Cagle's hand. Cagle's grip was firm, but not granite. Kinderstrom noted that Cagle made sure that he was standing two steps above him and thereby allow himself to appear superior to the man beneath him.

Cagle looked at the cowboy waiting patiently in the hallway and said, "You can go, Devery."

"Thanks, Mister Cagle." Then his eyes went to Kinderstrom; there was anger in them.

Kinderstrom just returned the look with a smirk, turned and followed Cagle up the stairs.

After they heard Devery close the front door, Cagle asked, "I saw the look Devery just gave you. Did you, by any chance, anger him in some way?"

Kinderstrom said wryly, "Is it my problem he doesn't like being called stupid?"

"I must warn you about Phil Devery. Under his crude and brainless exterior, is an extremely mean and sadistic man when he wants to be—especially with a bottle in his frequently dirty hands. If I were you, I'd give him a wide berth."

Kinderstrom was almost touched by this cold man's concern about him.

"Why, thank you."

"Don't thank me," Cagle said stiffly as he stopped on the second floor and looked down at him. "You're an important cog in the machinery by which Mister McDermott forms his plans. If anything should happen to you, the execution of those plans might be delayed, if not entirely thrown into disarray. We need your skills, not necessarily *you*. Do I make myself clear?"

Kinderstrom stared back at him, trying to hide his rage, and said, "Completely."

Not noticing Kinderstrom's anger, or not caring to, Cagle merely responded, "Good." Then he turned and continued down the hallway to the second door on his left. He knocked on it and the voice of a middle-aged man answered, "Yes, come in." The voice sounded irritable, as if he weren't in the mood to be disturbed.

Cagle opened the door and entered, with Kinderstrom following, hat in hand.

Tad McDermott sat behind his desk, a lit cigar between his teeth billowing up a cloud of smoke before his hooded eyes. He wore a dark suit that had seen better days, but due to the fact that it was rarely worn, it gave the appearance of being new. McDermott had to be in his fifties; he was balding on top, his light brown hair cropped short around his ears. The face was tanned by the sun and the creases around the mouth seemed to imply a man who scowled a great deal. His long nose was sharp, as if someone had chiseled it into a hawk-like beak. The brown eyes were slits, whether because of the cigar smoke before them or because they never fully opened, Kinderstrom couldn't tell. Even seated, one could tell that Tad McDermott was a tall man, wide in the chest, with thick, muscular arms and long fingers.

The fingers of a gunman, Kinderstrom surmised.

McDermott said, "Sit down, Kinderstrom."

Again, like the introduction to Len Cagle, it was hardly a greeting. McDermott didn't even rise to shake hands.

Obediently, Kinderstrom sat in a chair in front of the desk. Cagle remained standing.

After flicking a cigar ash towards a nearby ashtray on his desk

—and missing—McDermott said irritably, "I don't like puttin' on fancy suits for anyone, Kinderstrom, but I made an exception in this case."

Kinderstrom didn't know whether to be flattered or appalled. *Did everyone out west act like swine?*

"Let's can the fancy-pants pleasantries, and get right down to why you're here," said McDermott. He blew out a cloud of cigar smoke, not caring whether or not it floated into Kinderstrom's face. "You've handled land claims out in Stockholm with Swedish farmers."

"That's right," said Kinderstrom. "In your letters, you mentioned that there were similar cases here in Nebraska. Farmers and homesteaders claiming government land all over the state."

"Right. Back in Sweden, you were a popular man in the government. They say you were pretty close to the royal family and such."

Kinderstrom just nodded, not knowing where McDermott was going with this.

"You wrote in one of your letters that you were up for a minister post. Forget which one you said."

"Interior Minister."

"Yeah, that's right. But then some reform movement took over the government and squeezed your ass out."

Kinderstrom reddened at the crudeness of that statement. Reluctantly, he nodded in agreement.

McDermott leaned forward then, his small eyes shining when he said, "But when you were in your heyday, you and a combine of industrialists and land developers made a nice profit pushin' the farmers off their land."

Kinderstrom didn't know how to respond. Was the man indicting him or was he just going over his qualifications?

McDermott's next comment gave him his answer. Leaning back in his chair, he said, "*That's* the kind of man I need here in Nebraska. You know how to buy folks, Kinderstrom. You bought them in the imperial courts of Europe, and I don't think you'll have any trouble buyin' 'em here in America. Listen..." He leaned forward again, the cigar lowered to the surface of the desk; his gaze on Kinderstrom was steady. "All told, we're talkin' about a multi-million dollar business here. Me and my partners in the combine control thousands of acres of prime real estate out here. And I didn't get in this position by bein' nice to my neighbors either. Me and my partners did kind of what you and your partners did back in Sweden; takin' the land from folks who are just too stupid and too useless to know what to do with it. Hell, the homesteaders out here didn't fight for the land they're on, not like the way me and my crew did. We fought some damn hostile red niggers and drove 'em off with their tails between their legs before the first home-steader knew how to build a fence."

When Kinderstrom looked at him oddly, he sighed and added, "Indians."

"Oh..."

"Anyway, me and my partners are owners of some of the finest cattle in this country. Prime full-blooded stock, thousands of 'em. Kinderstrom, I don't exaggerate when I tell you that, if we wanted, we have the power to give life or take it. Right now, we're doin' the latter..."

Even as he listened to the statement and tried not to judge McDermott's crudeness and lack of tact, Kinderstrom couldn't help feeling a chill at the man's words.

"We've spent a lot of money to hire some help in cleanin' out the surroundin' valley. We've hired, I think some twenty-three or twenty-four fast guns to handle the job now, but it's bigger than even they can handle. So, our people have gone down to Texas to hire some more men. Once they're put on the payroll, they get five dollars a day, plus fifty for any homesteader they kill. Half that for the wives or any other womenfolk, and maybe five or ten for the kids."

Kinderstrom stared at him. He himself had hired gunmen to take care of some obstinate farmer or nester, but he had never hired anyone to murder their wives or children. He tried not to look appalled.

McDermott continued, "We've been sending our crew out all over the valley in groups of five to ten to take care of the homesteaders. All of them jaspers have built their cabins so far apart and are so absorbed in their own lives that they haven't organized yet—a lucky break for us. My boys hit 'em fast and hit 'em permanent, giving the settlers no time to rig up any kind of defense. I figure, in six months' time, maybe less, we will have wiped them out."

"And my part in all this?" he asked.

McDermott pointed a long finger at him and said, "Your part in all this is to twist the law into so many goddamn knots that it'll take a genius decades to untangle 'em!"

Now it was Kinderstrom's turn to lean forward; he listened intently.

Seeing his interest, McDermott responded animatedly. "You see," he explained, "back in sixty-two, our congress enacted a law called the Homestead Act. This law allows any American to own title to government land at no cost. They've got to build a house or a cabin or some such dwelling among some hundred sixty acres of prime land, farm it, and make improvements to the property within in a space of five years. In other words, they have to 'prove up' on the land. You have to be at least twenty-one years old, a veteran of the Union Army during the Civil War, or be designated a 'head of household', meanin' a woman by herself could own land also..." He paused to give a disgusted look. "Anyway, the situation was fine till a few years back. First, there were soldiers returnin' from the war comin' back and findin' their homes burned or whatever, so they go west to start fresh and they end up here. But the past ten years or so, you got these foreigners comin' here also. Ya know, folks that say they're lookin' for a new start from what they call religious prosecution."

Kinderstrom cleared his throat and said, "*Persecution*."

McDermott's eyes swung to him and said, "That's what I said!"

Kinderstrom didn't reply.

"Anyway, me and my partners can be a little plain-speakin' and, let's say we're not very subtle on how we deal with the public or government officials. We need a spokesman for our combine. A legal trouble-shooter and public relations man who'll make us look like saints and the other guys look like trash. Someone who'll take the Homestead Act and make it deader'n Abe Lincoln."

"This combine of yours; does it have a name?"

"Yeah. We call ourselves the Cattlemen's Association of Western Nebraska."

"C-A-W-N."

McDermott's eyes briefly looked upward thinking about it. Then he nodded and said, "Yeah, that's about right."

"Do you own the local constables here, as we do in Europe?"

"Some of 'em," he said off-handedly. "You still have a marshal or two in some town or other who actually respect their badges, but our people do their best to squeeze 'em out one way or the other. Guess these fellows don't think much about fattening their wallets any." He then shook his head and said, "Dumb bastards."

"When would you want me to start?"

"Right away. You told me what the landowners were payin' you back in Stockholm and let me tell you, it's a squirt o' tobacco juice in a spittoon compared to the money you'll get from us."

Kinderstrom didn't know whether to be elated by the offer or disgusted by the imagery behind it.

McDermott said, "You'll take your orders directly from Len. He used to ride with Quantrill back in Sixty-three. Told me they threw a hell of a party in Lawrence, Kansas when he was a little shaver with just a single-action Navy pistol for a friend."

Kinderstrom turned around and looked at Cagle. There was no expression on his face at all; Kinderstrom had no way of knowing whether he was embarrassed by McDermott's words, or angry or whatever. His face was an impassive mask.

"Everything clear, Kinderstrom?"

Kinderstrom turned back to face him.

"Very much, sir."

McDermott's smile told Kinderstrom that he liked being called "sir".

"That's it in a nutshell, Kinderstrom," he said, crushing out the stub of his cigar on the desk. Kinderstrom noticed that he missed the ashtray again.

Then McDermott's eyes bore into Kinderstrom's, and his expression became deadly serious.

"This state is growin' faster than your eyes can blink, and so's the rest of the country. We're not waitin' for this land to become hearth and home to every Mick and Jew-boy from the east. We're takin' up roots now. And God help any mother's son who gets in our way..."

Hiram Semple finally stood erect and wiped the sweat off his balding head as he took a breather from digging. He stared at the ditch he had commenced to digging a week ago and wondered if irrigation was all it was made out to be. Yet that was part of the stipulations in the Homestead Act; irrigating the land was part and parcel of land ownership; "proving up" meant back-breaking toil with little time to sit back and enjoy the land he had just been granted. *Damn federals*, he thought, still using the term he had used since he was a soldier in rebel gray at the age of sixteen. *They don't do any American any favors unless a body kills himself.* He wondered just who was doing who a favor, since it was himself and thousands of homesteaders who were building on and improving the land while the government sits back and pretends it's so generous and charitable.

Semple set aside the shovel and went over to a wooden chair he had brought along with him and put under the shade of a nearby cottonwood. When his rear end hit the seat, he felt like he didn't want to rise again, ever. He exhaled and tried not to stare at the ditch; it would only remind him of how far he had yet to go. Instead, he looked up at the leaves overhead and got to thinking about what he had accomplished so far. It was mid-April and though there was still a chill in the air, his work had made him overheated, and sweat clung to his worn overalls. He figured that there was water further down the bend, the closer he got to Pawnee Creek. If he was able to divert some of that water, he might be able to have his own creek right near his cabin. And if the rains came frequently in a couple months, he might be able to dam the water and use the location to attract weary travelers coming through the area; an oasis in the middle of nowhere, especially with the nearest town being thirty miles away. Maybe he could even open up a place that served food and refreshments.

He smiled at the thought.

He sat forward and was about to rise off the chair when he heard the hoof beats in the distance. He frowned at the noise, wondering who would be visiting him in the middle of his work. After all, his closest neighbor, some cattleman with the oddball name of Eugene Cornelius Farnsworth, wasn't anywhere near his property.

Listening to the approaching riders, Semple suddenly got nervous. There was no mistaking it; there were a *lot* of riders approaching. In fact, he hadn't heard so many horses approach him since the federals tried to charge his position at Bull Run.

He got up slowly from his chair. When he finally saw the riders, they had literally surrounded him. Semple looked around and saw them walking their mounts in and out of the trees. They appeared as if they were searching for someone; or perhaps just making sure he was alone.

One particular rider trotted up in front of Semple and looked down at him as if he were a rattlesnake that had just popped up in the trail to spook his horse. The man had his black Stetson pulled down tight on his forehead and its brim seemed to be pointing at Semple. The brown eyes, which seemed coal black when it caught snatches of sunlight filtering down through the trees, were small but piercing; Semple would not want to get into a staring match with this man. His black mustache was thick and covered most of his small mouth; it also complimented the crisp, clean black shirt and brown cowhide vest he wore. The man didn't scowl at Semple, but the look on his tanned face was cold. The man scared him, yet he couldn't tear his gaze away.

Semple was just about to inquire what was wrong—he *knew* that the men were not here on a friendly visit—when the man before him beat him to it.

"Hiram Semple," the man said, with a curt drawl.

"Yes," he answered.

"That your cabin back yonder?"

"Yeah. What the hell's going o—"

"Well, you built that cabin on someone else's property."

Semple responded with a word indicating that it was a lie.

The man just looked at him, his horse stepping forward to crowd Semple back against the tree.

"Hey," he said, putting up his hands to shove the horse's head away. "Keep your damn horse's head away from me!"

The man leaned down in the saddle and said quietly, "If I were you, mister, I wouldn't worry about his *face*."

Semple's gray eyes looked up at him uncomprehendingly.

Then, after the man jabbed his horse's right flank with his spur, the animal suddenly rose off his two forelegs with a painful whinny. Backed against the tree, Semple was frightened and confused and totally unprepared for what happened next. When the horse brought his hoofs back to earth, his right hoof slashed down and struck Semple's face, dislocating his jaw in the process. Semple cried out and slid down the tree to the ground, holding his bleeding mouth.

Still leaning forward in the saddle, the man calmly said. "Took a fellow I hired the longest time to teach him that. Aren't you impressed?"

Semple's reply was a tearful whine as blood dripped down his overalls.

"No?" the man said. Then he leaned back and commenced a conversation with his horse.

"That's a shame, Fred. This man doesn't appreciate your hand-iwork. Let's teach 'em a lesson."

To Semple's horror, the horse rose again off his forelegs and this time, came down square on his head. The man made his horse repeat the move several times, crushing Semple's skull beneath its hooves.

"Charlie!" called one of the riders. The man then rode up to the tree and said, "He died five minutes ago. You're gonna tire ol' Fred out."

Charlie Quinn turned to look at the man and said, "Just makin' sure, Al. Anyway, 'ol Fred could use the exercise. You find anyone else on the property?"

Al Hardy shook his head and said, "Not a soul."

"Good."

"Should we burn the cabin?"

Quinn pulled out the makings and started to roll himself a cigarette.

"Dunno yet.   Figure Gene Farnsworth could use it for something."

"That dirty shack? What's he gonna use it for?"

"Don't rightly know.   Maybe he'll invite some of his high-fallutin' friends to use it for a new 'gentlemen's club' or something."

Hardy chuckled with a raspy sound that grated on the ears. Then he said, "Like to see those high-hats live one day in that rat trap. They'd be runnin' back to the big city just to wipe their noses."

"Maybe," said Quinn, exhaling some smoke in the cool country air.

"Where to next?"

"List says some jasper some forty or so miles west of Pawnee Creek."

"You gonna give Fred some more exercise?"

"Naw, I figure the boys need some target practice. Some of them'll start to get rusty."

"That'll *never* happen."

"Got an idea. Take Bill and Ed and ride over to the Bingham place. Kill two birds with one stone."

"All right. I wouldn't mind payin' a visit to ol' George. Understand he needs the company since his wife died and all."

"Yeah, and I want you to do something else."

"What?"

"Hell with it. Burn it down..."

The rider barreled down the main street of Starrett City, her horse already building up foam in its coat. Passersby stopped and stared at her as she sped by.

One man said, "Paul Revere warnin' us about the British?"

"Nah," said his companion. "Just that damn Carmody woman with a broomstick up her butt again."

Jill Carmody could only imagine what the people on the boardwalks were saying about her—again. She had been through it all before and was always hurt by their scorn, and in turn, she always hated them for their ignorance, their laziness and their almost neurotic need to avoid any social responsibility and keep their collective noses out of trouble.

Jill was wearing her brother's wool shirt, a pair of Levi's and a pair of scuffed brown riding boots given her by her father on her eighteenth birthday. She was also wearing a brown cotton vest which was open and flapping in the wind as she rode past. To the men watching her from the sidewalk, seeing Jill's tall, gangling frame in the saddle, with her honey-blonde hair blown back on her head as she rode past them, she was a striking figure; so different from their prim and proper wives and their corsets and bustles and their hair piled up on their heads with old hairpins or pulled back severely into a ponytail. They could even see themselves desiring such a woman.

Now if only she wasn't such a pain in the butt.

Jill brought her horse to a stop in front of the jail, pulled her feet out of the stirrups and dropped to the ground with a quick movement. After tying the reins to the hitching rail, she mounted the walk just in time to be met by Marshal Rawlins coming out of his office.

He nodded at her and said, "Heard you comin' up the street. Afternoon, Ma'am."

Winded from her long ride, she spoke rapidly, taking breaths between sentences. Rawlins noted wryly that it was the way Jill Carmody *always* talked, winded or not.

"Marshal," she said, "there's another fire in the Pawnee Creek area. Maybe thirty miles off the creek. I'd say it was somewhere close to Hiram Semple's place, but I'm not sure. He lives pretty far from us. Anyway, this is the fifth one in a week. I'd just like to know what you're going to do about it."

The marshal paused and wryly asked, "And how are you, Miss Carmody?"

Her hazel eyes grew narrow. She had taken this before as well, all too many times.

"Don't patronize me, Marshal. I'm not in the mood."

Rawlins tried not to smirk when he said, "And what *would* you be in the mood for, Miss Carmody?"

He then leered at her, his tongue almost touching his teeth. He couldn't help it; this filly *had* to be brought down some day.

"You're a pig, Rawlins."

"Yes, Ma'am," he said, grinning. "At your service."

"I've been riding into town practically every other day to report these incidents and you've just stood there and grinned at me. You should be replaced."

Rawlins sighed and said, "You're right, Miss Carmody—as usual. I *should* be replaced. But right now, I'm the only law you've got. And as far as I'm concerned, 'taint a cloud of black smoke in the sky over Pawnee Creek. You must be mistaken."

"And what about the bodies?"

Rawlins gave himself a look of surprise. To Jill, it was bad playacting and she rolled her eyes when she saw it.

"Bodies? Why, Miss Carmody, what bodies are you talkin' about?"

"The bodies Morg and I found on the O'Connor place the other day."

"Oh yes," he said agreeably, "*those* bodies."

Jill looked at him incredulously and said, "Are you *drunk*? If you got up off your fat butt and rode out to the far end of the valley, you'd know what I was talking about."

The marshal looked at her coolly, but there was rage behind his eyes.

"Now, Miss Carmody," he said, with feigned patience, "you're startin' to make me forget that your pa and I are friends."

Jill smiled gravely at him and said, "No, Marshal, not friends, *collaborators!*"

She turned around and went to the tie rail. After untying the reins, she climbed into the saddle and rode off back up the street.

Marshal Rawlins remained leaning against a post, watching her lean figure disappear out of view. He shook his head ruefully. *All that woman and no man anywhere near her but that surly brother of hers. Wonder what she does when she's lonely...*

Tom Asch, the *Sentinel's* typesetter, passed by and said, "Afternoon, Marshal."

"Afternoon, Tom. Hey, wait a minute!"

Asch stopped and looked at him.

"You're a smart fella, Tom. You've got to be, on your job."

"What's on your mind?"

Rawlins paused and then asked, "What's a...*col-lab-or-ator?*"

It was a full hour and forty minutes before George Bingham woke up with the biggest headache in the world. Added to his headache, it seemed that the world was bouncing up and down. Bouncing up and down and totally pitch black.

It took a little while before he shook himself fully awake and realized that his face was touching a black burlap bag that had been pulled over the top half of his body. It was a moth-eaten cloth bag you'd find in a general store and it stank of old potatoes. He tried to raise his hands and found that they had been tied behind his back.

Then, to his surprise, the horse under him stopped.

A pair of leather-gloved hands loosened the rope that held him to the saddle and roughly pulled him off. His body, already aching all over, hit the ground with a thud. In fact, he noted ruefully, he had made impact with a rock surface.

He heard a voice then say, "Take it off."

George was roughly pulled up to his knees and two pairs of hands yanked the old sack off him, the men doing the yanking not caring about taking some of George's face and hair with the sack as they pulled it off.

After he blinked his eyes at the sun overhead, he looked down and noticed that dried blood had stained his calico shirt. It was probably from the pistol-whipping he had endured earlier.

He looked to his right and saw Al Hardy leaning his lean frame against a boulder with a big smile on his tanned face. Casually, he rolled a cigarette as he spoke.

"Glad you're back with us, George."

Still on his knees, Bingham said angrily, "What kind of goddamn robbery is this, Hardy? You could've taken my belongings, my horses, anything you wanted, but did you have to conk me on the head and bring me all the way out here too?"

"Now, now, George," said Hardy lazily, "is that any way to act? I understand that the Bingham name still means something in these parts."

Bingham eyed him bitterly. He'd have to bring that up, wouldn't he?

Hardy took a drag of his cigarette and said, "If you had played ball with us long ago, you wouldn't be out here now. You'd be sittin' up at the Cattlemen's House sippin' champagne and smokin' the finest cigars. But *no*! You have to grow yourself a pair of angel wings and float right up to heaven!"

Bingham's anger grew. He didn't like being made fun of by some sawed-off little cowpuncher in dirty chaps.

"You through with your sick game, Hardy, or are you going to bore me to death as well?"

Hardy's eyes became little slits. He wasn't even pretending to be jovial now. He gave a curt nod to the two men. They bent over and yanked Bingham to his feet. Then they pulled his struggling form over to the edge of a bluff.

"Look down, George," Hardy ordered. "Look down *real good*!"

Bingham's eyes looked over the edge and he saw a chasm that seemed bottomless. His booted feet scraped against the edge and several pebbles went over into the abyss below. He couldn't see where they ended up.

"I'm not playin' any games with you now, George."

Bingham was frightened. He had heard that McDermott's men were crazy, but he didn't realize the depth of their insanity until this very moment, with his life a fraction of an inch away from eternity.

George cried, "Jesus Christ, Hardy! What the hell are you doing?!"

"Doing?" asked Hardy, leaning forward. "Why, I'm gettin' rid of a *cancer*!"

George said, "You even sound like old Tad! The way he treats folks who are in his way, like a disease."

Hardy said grimly, "One quick question, George, before Bill and Ed step back and you step forward. We know your wife died some years ago, but we heard talk of a son. Some jasper back in New York City or some such place. Is that true?"

Bingham's face became a mask. When he thought of his son, he almost forgot about the edge of the cliff.

Bingham said tightly, "I have no son."

"You sure, George? I mean, you didn't happen to forget, did ya?"

"Shut up, Hardy!"

"Gotta ask, George. Because, ya see, if you had a son, by rights he could come out here and claim your property. Now I'll ask ya again—"

George shouted, "Are you stupid, Hardy, or do you just look stupid! I told you, *I have no son!*"

Hardy eyes narrowed and he said quietly, "I don't like bein' called stupid, George..."

He nodded at the two men and they stepped back while at the same time gave Bingham a little shove.

The tied-up man went over the edge and his screams echoed back up the canyon as he plummeted down the cliff's face.

Hardy paused to listen. Then he said, "Sounds kinda pretty, don't it?"

Bill and Ed looked over the side and watched the falling man disappear to the bottom.

"Jesus," exclaimed Ed, almost in wonder. "I never did hear anyone scream like that."

Bill said, "You try huntin' Apaches up in the Dragoons some time. They'd tie up some Mexican girl they kidnapped and lower her head-first into a fire. Now *that's* a scream."

"Huh!"

"Where to now, Al?"

Hardy answered, "The Willoughby farm. A few miles over the ridge." Then he flicked an ash to the ground, indicated the cliff and said, "By the way, this fifty is *mine*."

Bill protested, "Now hold on, Al. Ed and I did the shovin'. We figure it's a good twenty-five apiece for each of us."

Hardy said, "Yeah, but *I* ordered you to do it, makin' *me* responsible for the kill. That fifty is *mine!*"

Bill and Ed looked at each other, then faced Hardy with stony expressions. Both men were tensed for trouble, their hands not far from their guns.

Ed said, "We hate to differ with you, Al, but Bill and me don't see it that way."

Hardy stared at them both and then grinned.

He said agreeably, "Guess you're right, Ed. You boys deserve the money."

The two men relaxed.

Bill said, "We don't want this comin' between us, Al."

Hardy said, "Neither do I."

Then he drew his gun with such speed that the two men barely had a chance to be shocked by the move. A bullet pierced the lining of Bill's stomach, then another hit Ed in the chest. Both men doubled over and then toppled back over the edge. Their twin screams could be heard for miles until their bodies passed the lower reaches of the chasm and finally hit the bottom.

Holstering his smoking gun, Hardy said, "Too bad you boys weren't worth anything. I hate workin' for free..."

CHAPTER TWO

THE CATTLEMEN'S HOUSE WAS SITUATED AT THE END OF THIRD Street and stood as a kind of sentinel between the town and the open prairie. It was four stories high which not only made it the tallest building in town, but its heavy wooden façade implied a culture and elegance missing from the rest of the town's architecture. The inside had plush red carpeting, wall to wall in fact, and the couches and chairs were covered in genuine velour upholstery. Matching the carpet, the various windows were adorned by red floor-to-ceiling curtains. There was a room for practically every game or leisure one could think of; a card room, a billiard room, a reading room; and, of course, a lounge on the top floor where the cattlemen could have a drink or a cigar while they talked business.

The fourth floor, the one with the main lounge, had a huge kitchen where French chefs, basically imported from Canada, turned out sumptuous meals for the members of the Combine and their guests. The servants themselves wore spotless white uniforms and were models of cleanliness down to their well-trimmed fingernails. Their duties were to make the cattlemen happy; to serve them the various imported wines, cognacs and liqueurs from their well-stocked kitchen, to serve them their meals, and even to light their cigars.

Transporting the members to the fourth-floor lounge was an electric-powered elevator, one of the few in the territory. When the building was erected, Tad McDermott had insisted on its installation; he and his partners were not going to climb stairs if he could help it. It was powered by an electric motor on the bottom of the car and propelled up and down under thick cables; a young man named Kenneth operated it from within the car and God help him if he wasn't there when someone wanted it. The trip was sometimes slow going, but it was better than climbing all those steps; all CAWN's members were over fifty.

The building itself was McDermott's idea; he had it built with the Combine's money for use as a combination headquarters and playground. No ordinary townsmen were allowed to enter; this was an ironclad rule laid down by the CAWN's well-fed and financially comfortable members.

Tad McDermott sat in the fourth-floor lounge and smoked a huge and quite smelly cigar, a snifter of brandy at his elbow. The cigar smoke from the other smelly cigars in the room hung like an oppressive cloud, but it seemed that the other men were used to it.

McDermott had just had a huge pheasant for dinner and topped it off with an imported French wine. The other four men in the circle of plush chairs had had equally rich dinners and were smoking equally smelly cigars. They were in fine suit coats, pressed black trousers and boiled shirts. McDermott just wore a brown suit and string tie. He liked the club's ambience, especially their food and wine, but he always hated dressing up and did so only because the club rules prohibited anyone to be there without a tie. And of course, in order to have a tie, he had to wear a suit as well. Powerful as he was, he had to give in to his partners' demands for formal attire. He decided to let them have this little carrot since he dominated them in so many other ways.

"The pheasant was *excellent* tonight, wasn't it, Peter?"

This was Honus Wilder, a former railroad man from Chicago. Though his rather huge belly made him seem soft and he looked too frail for the west, back in Chicago he was the man to whom scabs went to for steady employment in the event that any talk of unions rose up in the rail yards of the south side. This usually occurred due to Wilder's insistence on keeping his workers' wages somewhere below that of seamstress; if anyone complained, the complainer usually got a blackjack slammed into his skull courtesy of Honus Wilder's well-paid private security force. Ultimately, weary of battling labor organizers and eastern reformers, he decided to move west and invest in cattle.

Pete Ridgeway smiled and answered, "Excellent as usual, Honus."

Peter Hollingworth Ridgeway, of the Philadelphia Ridgeways, arrived in cattle country with a price on his huge aging head. He was a manufacturer of wagons and buckboards. Told one day by his foreman that his stock was infested with termites, Ridgeway shrugged off the report and promptly fired his foreman. Then it was discovered that families traveling through Indian country had their wagons suddenly collapse under them, leaving them stranded in the middle of nowhere and forced to fend off the various tribes who inhabited the area.

A jury indicted him for fraud, negligence and manslaughter. However, somewhere along the way, money exchanged hands and Ridgeway's thirty-year sentence was reduced to a fine; needless to say, the amount paid never made it to the local treasury.

Judge James Alcott remarked that the *turkey* cooked the previous night by their French chef Francois was still the best thing he had ever tasted. Judge Alcott, as one can tell from his title, was a jurist of some years who had sat on the bench in Putnam County in upstate New York. Yet it was his activities in his chambers with a pretty young barmaid from Rochester that drew the attention of the state bar. Arrested for propositioning men at an "an ungodly hour" near the waterfront, the young lady was promised her freedom by Judge Alcott if she joined him in his chambers after the building was officially closed for the day. Unfortunately, a porter discovered them when he attempted to clean the chambers. Alcott was banished from sitting on a New York State judge's bench but was not barred from being part of some other judicial system somewhere west of the Mississippi. It was his job to routinely throw out any and all cases brought against the cattlemen by some angry homesteader. As a reward for his loyalty to their cause, they added to his ranch some of their best cows, and for free.

Eugene Cornelius Farnsworth wasn't listening to the men talk about food; he was watching the young blonde waitress serve the men across the room. Though it was a men's club, some of the members insisted on being served by pretty, young women in French maid outfits. The establishment's butlers were against the idea, but they didn't own the building; the cattlemen did. Farnsworth had an eye for the ladies, and to his discerning eye, the younger the better. His own long-suffering wife of twenty-one years was a tall, blonde-haired woman of good figure and better sexual appetites—or at least she used to be. Then one day, Farnsworth came home and found her in the arms of his partner in the textile business they owned in Trenton, New Jersey. Two gunshots later, the pair was lying in bed soaked in blood and Farnsworth claimed that young Halstead and his wife must have made a suicide pact. With a gun planted in the bed with Halstead's finger around the trigger, authorities seemed helpless to prove otherwise.

Still, it was tough trying to explain to his little daughter Jill just why mommy was not around anymore, and why daddy kept getting fingers pointed at him on the street.

Two months later, Farnsworth married one of the girls in his factory, a handsome brunette named Veronica Carmody, who was already the mother of a little boy named Morgan. There were rumors that "Ronnie," as Tyler liked to call her, wasn't married when she had the boy.

Bad memories, and even worse rumors, all justified, were indeed strong. To have his new wife called a whore was one thing, but to be whispered about as a murderer was *especially* not good for business; and so, Farnsworth sold out his factory holdings and, after Ronnie's untimely death from a fall down a flight of stairs, took his family and went west. Cattle was bigger business than textiles anyway, especially far away from New Jersey.

Ridgeway nodded cheerfully and said, "The turkey *was* good, Judge, but the pheasant was *superb*! What do you think, Theodore?"

McDermott winced at the name. He hadn't been called Theodore since the vicar at his old parish whipped the bejesus out of him for being caught with little Agnes Collins behind the rectory of St. Bernard's in Baltimore.

He replied, "I don't give a goddamn about the food in this place, and I didn't call you men here to discuss your goddamn stomachs!"

The three men nearest him tried to look dismayed, but inwardly they smirked. Good old Tad, always bringing the rest of them, kicking and screaming, off their high horses and back to earth.

As usual, McDermott didn't beat around the bush.

"Hardy tells me he killed George Bingham the other day."

Ridgeway said, "My God!"

Wilder shook his head and said, "That's a shame."

Farnsworth tore his eyes from the blonde waitress across the room and said, "Huh?"

McDermott gruffly said, "Glad you're with us, Gene. Now if you can forget that little blonde tart and pay attention, then maybe we can get down to business."

Wilder asked, "How'd it happen?"

McDermott replied, "Hardy said he shot George and shoved his body over the cliff at Raymond's Bend. We owe him fifty for it."

Farnsworth asked suspiciously, "Do you believe him?"

"'Course not. Charlie Quinn reported to me that two of his men, Bill Daggett and Ed Herrara, lit out some time last night. But the others tell me that if they did, they lit out without their horses, saddles and gear. To me, this means that Al Hardy probably killed old Bill and Ed when they tried to horn in on his profits. Maybe he shot 'em, maybe he threw 'em off the cliff right along with George, I don't know. Either way, Charlie Quinn's his pal and was coverin' up for him."

Wilder asked, "Well, shouldn't Hardy be fired?"

"For *what?*" McDermott asked, his voice rising. "For being a good businessman? Hell, if those two cowpokes tried to horn in on *my* killin' fee, I would've shot 'em too!"

Judge Alcott shook his head and said, "Poor George. What a way to die. To be thrown off a cliff."

McDermott said, "Better him than *us*, gentlemen. He was a good man. He worked hard for the Combine, harder than any of us put together—'ceptin' me that is." The others weren't smiling, for they knew that McDermott wasn't joking. He had an inflated opinion of himself, and none of the others had the guts to bring *him* down to earth.

He continued, "George was our friend. He twisted the law for us, and we made him rich. But then he turns against us, gets rid of his holdings and goes to live out on the flats with the home-steaders and take up their cause. Gentlemen, I can't stand traitors! As far as I'm concerned, that cliff he was pushed off of wasn't high enough!"

The rest of them were silent. They had all seen Tad McDer-mott when he was angry, but he was positively vindictive now.

He added, "As to the subject of George Bingham, I call it closed and good riddance. Let the wolves at the bottom of that drop worry about 'em...Oh, by the way, Gene. That was a good idea getting rid of that Semple character. Give him another six months and he would've diverted Pawnee Creek to his property. The place was too close to your range, anyway."

Farnsworth said, "Thanks, Tad."

Deep down, he knew that Charlie Quinn would never have raided Semple's property and murdered him at *his* orders. The twenty-five gunmen they had, and the newly arrived men hired from a trip to Texas, were under the direct orders of Tad McDer-mott and no one else.

"Now, on another topic," McDermott said expansively. "I told you about Ches Kinderstrom. He's going to be our liaison to the state's power brokers. Also, I just put him in charge of running the *Sentinel*, like George used to do."

Alcott asked, "Can he run a newspaper?"

"Probably not, but experience doesn't matter when you run a newspaper. All we want is for the paper to sing our praises and give the public a load of crap. Otherwise, you could take 'journal-istic integrity' and shove it up your ass. Integrity doesn't pay the bills.

"Now to another matter. Gene, it's that goddamn crazy daughter of yours."

Farnsworth closed his eyes briefly, then opened them and stared at McDermott.

"Go on, Tad. What's she done now?"

"Rawlins tells me she rode into town hell bent for leather and filed another complaint about the boys burnin' cabins up north. Listen, I tell Charlie Quinn to lay off her 'cause she's your daughter, but if she sticks her nose in our business more directly, I won't be responsible for a bullet accidentally fired in her direction; you savvy?"

Farnsworth grimaced. He didn't like another man threatening his daughter, but Tad McDermott wasn't just another man.

When Farnsworth didn't respond right away, McDermott said, "Damn it, Gene! She's *your* daughter! Can't you hustle her butt out of town or something?"

Farnsworth said, "She hasn't spoken to me in a year and you know it."

Judge Alcott leaned forward in his chair and said, "My God, Gene, doesn't she realize that we can put her on easy street for the rest of her days? If she played along with us, she won't have to live in that grimy two-room shack with your son—"

Farnsworth said sharply, "He's *not* my son!"

Alcott said, "Sorry, Gene."

"That's right," said Wilder, with a smirk. "Jill's so ashamed of you, she even took her stepbrother's last name, didn't she?"

Farnsworth glared at him and seemed about to explode until McDermott cut in.

"I don't care whose son or whose daughter gets in our hair," he said irritably. "Just *do* something about it! You hear me, Gene? Or it'll force us to take measures. And you know me and my boys don't do anything halfway."

Farnsworth paused for a moment, and then said, "I hear you, Tad."

"Good. Now another matter of business is George Bingham's kin."

Wilder said, "But I thought his wife died of fever years ago."

"I don't mean his wife," growled McDermott. "I mean his son."

"He has a son?" said Ridgeway. "He never mentioned one."

"Well, he's got one. My people back east tell me he's a paper pusher in New York. They're goin' through a poor economic spell back east, and it hit them pretty hard. So, it seems our boy was let go from his firm along with hundreds of other folks. My contacts tell me that one Jerome Bingham took a westbound train from New York about a week ago. He'll transfer to other trains, and then a stage and he should be here maybe tomorrow, weather and train schedules permittin'."

Wilder asked, "Why is he coming out here? George hardly mentioned him."

Farnsworth said, "Perhaps the boy has nowhere to go now that he's out of a job and New York's in an economic slump. Maybe he seeks a rapprochement with his father."

"Maybe," agreed Judge Alcott.

"*Rapprochement!*" said McDermott loudly. "Yeah, I'd like to see him reunite with his old man now!"

The others tried to ignore McDermott's crude snicker and focus on the matter.

Ridgeway leaned forward in his chair and asked, "Did George have a chance to send his son a letter or some other communication asking him to come?"

"Maybe," McDermott answered. "We told Bart Johnson to let us know if any telegram went out that might get us in hot water, but so far he hasn't spotted anything."

Ridgeway said, "But if George traveled to Omaha and somehow posted a letter from there, we have no way of controlling the mail traffic from that point. A letter could have conceivably gone through asking his son to come here."

"That's possible," McDermott agreed. "Those jaspers up in Omaha don't like playin' by our rules. Bunch of stinkin' choir boys run the show up there, if ya ask me."

"Well, what do we do?" asked Judge Alcott. "The boy might try to file legal claim on George's land. As the only living blood relative, he has that right."

"Maybe he does," said McDermott gravely, "but mark my words: If he is comin' out here to lay claim to that land, he's gonna know what the 'blood' in blood relative means..."

The bullet splattered the old bottle which sat upon a boulder not far from their cabin. The ground at the foot of the boulder was littered with glass splinters and rusty, perforated tin cans.

He watched the last one splatter without any feeling. After all, it was just an empty rye bottle which had no use to anyone except as a target. Yet he knew that it would not have made any difference to him whether the bullet had splattered a bottle or the skull of a man—especially a certain kind of man.

He opened the gun and spun the cylinder of the wooden-handled Colt .45, punching out the spent shells and quickly reloading it with new ones. He snapped it shut expertly and started to aim again, this time towards the far-right end where other helpless containers awaited their end.

He heard the galloping hoofs behind him without fear. He just cocked the trigger and aimed. One shot later, another bottle splattered into infamy.

The horse stopped a few feet behind his left shoulder and a sardonic female voice spoke.

"You through yet?"

"In a minute," he answered.

She sighed and tried to sound patient but failed.

"Are you going to litter the backyard with glass splinters and tin cans all day, or are you going to do something *constructive* like, oh, digging that irrigation ditch?"

"Leave me be, Jill. Just a few minutes more."

Jill said tightly, "Jesus, Morg! She's been dead the better part of a year now; how long are you gonna mourn?"

She saw him stiffen at the remark. It was time to play the soothing mom again, as she had when he was a little boy.

She said gently, "I'm trying to be understanding, Morg. But the bitter avenger pose is getting on my nerves. Coming out here to practice your aim every goddamn day, shooting bottles to smithereens, never cracking a smile at the dinner table, jabbing your horse's butt with your spurs till the poor thing bleeds. I mean, I still love you, Morg, but now I'm also scared of you."

Morgan turned around and looked at her, the gun still in his right hand.

Her voice was a whisper, and tears were welling up in her eyes.

"I just want my brother back."

They just looked at each other for a few seconds more, and then she turned her horse and rode away.

Morgan stood there and watched her ride off. Then he looked at the gun in his hand, and finally holstered it.

He had just two carpetbags with him when he got off the train, then hired a buggy to take him into Starrett City. He got out in front of the Palmer Hotel and, after getting his bags, found himself looking up at its false front. It was two stories high and looked as ordinary as the rest of the block.

Two young women passed him on the boardwalk and smiled flirtatiously. He nodded and they giggled as they passed. He knew he wasn't a bad-looking man. He was just 25 years old, and though he was tall and square-shouldered, the sandy-haired man was not what the townsfolk would have called rugged. In fact, the three-piece suit, string tie and shined leather shoes he wore marked him as a "dude". The derby hat only verified that opinion.

After he signed the register, Sam Boston, who had been with the hotel when it first opened around the time of Gettysburg, spun the book around and looked at the page.

His small gray eyes looked up at him.

"Jerome Bingham."

Jerry looked at him, wondering why his name should be repeated out loud.

"That's right," he said, with a marked eastern accent.

Boston scratched his ear, which at his 76 years, was already covered with white hair.

"Any relation to George Bingham?"

He paused, then answered, "He's my father."

Boston blinked his ancient eyes and also paused. This was going to be tough.

"Have you...uh, have you heard about your father?"

Jerry eyed him suspiciously and said, "No. What about my father?"

Boston looked away briefly and said, "Oh boy."

Jerry asked, more urgently this time, "I said, what about my father?"

The old man reached into a wooden slot behind him and yanked out a key. He shoved it into Jerry's hand and said, "Here's your key. Room sixteen, second floor." He bustled around the counter as fast as his old legs could carry him. "I just remembered. Gotta check about a message at the telegraph office. Enjoy your stay."

Jerry watched him go, not wanting to physically grab the old man and press him for details. Boston left the hotel quickly, figuring to return in a few minutes and hoping that someone else would give Jerry the news about his father by the time he got back.

Jerry went up to his room and threw open the bags. He hung his clothes in the closet and then went over to the basin on the cupboard, poured a pitcher of water in and then threw the water all over his face and head. It was a long trip and he needed to sleep. *There would be time to see the old man later.* His tiredness was already making him forget the little clerk's odd behavior concerning his father.

Then, while drying his hands, he turned back towards the bed and saw that he had forgotten to unpack one thing in his second bag. He went over to it, reached in, and pulled out an 1877 Colt double-action army revolver. He cracked open the gate and checked the loads. Then he snapped the gun shut and shoved it into a shoulder holster he would wear under his coat.

He was hoping he wouldn't have to use it.

Jerry slept for a few hours and then washed up, dressed and went down for dinner.

As he ate, he asked the waitress about his father and she said she didn't know anyone named George Bingham. Yet he knew she was lying by how uncomfortable she looked when he asked the question. The steak he had was very thick, which is what he expected from a steak served in cattle country. After he finished, he sipped his coffee and sat back, watching the people who entered and left the room through the high archway which bridged the hotel and the restaurant.

Simple people, he thought. Seemingly so carefree and uncomplicated compared with the hustle-bustle of New York. He sighed and all at once got homesick. He hoped that his father was once again the same man he had known as a boy--the man who wasn't an overpaid errand boy for the cattle interests. It was the reason he hadn't spoken to him in so long.

But then again, he himself had been an overpaid representative for Wall Street lawyers; defending crooked executives and other such rabble from being indicted and sent far away to some upstate New York prison where they could probably be crooked there as well.

As he sat there, he thanked God that the law caught up with his firm and forced it to go under. If he hadn't played it straight as an arrow and saw to it that he didn't personally profit from his bosses' corrupt practices, he would be languishing in a cell in Elmira along with the firm's partners right at that moment.

Jerry was finishing his coffee when he glanced over at the next table and spotted the folded newspaper lying on the chair. The waitress who served him saw what he was looking at and quickly moved to clean the table and remove the newspaper.

But Jerry saw her coming and quickly grabbed it off the chair.

He saw the anger in her eyes then.

Turning away from her, he sat down again and opened the newspaper to the front page.

What he saw made him die inside...

The *Starrett City Sentinel* was on the first floor of a building on 2nd Street, two blocks from the Palmer Hotel. A huge glass window covered the front of the printing shop and the words *Starrett City Sentinel, the Last Word in Journalizm* had been painted in huge red letters. However, Journalism was spelled with a "z". It seemed that proofreading was not one of the paper's main virtues.

Jerry barged through the glass-paned door the newspaper crumpled in his hand. He stopped when he saw Jill Carmody standing before the front counter. She turned around and Jerry was stunned when he saw her face. She was tall, a honey-blonde whose hair hung down to her shoulders and she wore a man's shirt and trousers beneath a cotton vest. Her hazel eyes regarded him curiously. To Jerry, he had never seen a woman more striking than this one. Something about her almost made him forget what he was there for. No woman in all New York had ever looked like this.

He was starting to appreciate the beauty of Nebraska.

There was something about Jerry that Jill found vaguely familiar, though she couldn't put her finger on it then. She pulled her gaze away from him and turned around to once again face Tom Asch, the Sentinel's veteran typesetter. Asch compulsively straightened his visor, as he always did when addressing the public, and looked at Jill through dusty old glasses perched on his nose.

"I'm sorry, Ma'am," he said irritably, "but I don't write the stories, I just print 'em!"

"Oh really?" Jerry said angrily. Then he waved the crumpled paper in Asch's face and said, "What about calling my father the leader of a gang of rustlers? And saying that he was killed while resisting arrest?"

Jill stared at him then with a sudden realization.

She said quietly, "Oh my God."

Jerry looked at her.

"I see the resemblance now. You're George Bingham's son." Then she added, "I'm so sorry."

Jerry blinked his eyes rapidly and tried not to succumb to his grief in front of her. He had something to settle with these newspaper people; that took precedence.

He said gently, "Thank you, Miss."

"Mister Bingham..."

Jerry turned to Asch.

"I'm also sorry about your father, but if you wave that crumpled newspaper in my face again, gentleman or no gentleman, I will pop you one on the jaw, so help me God."

Jerry glared at him, wondering if it was worth getting into a fight with this idiot.

"Now if you'll excuse me," said Asch curtly, "I have work to do." He started to turn away.

"I bet you do, Mister Asch," Jill said bitterly. "Printing more lies for Tad McDermott and his trained dogs in the Combine."

Asch turned back to the counter and glared at her.

"Like I said, Miss Carmody, I'm a gentleman, but if it were up to me, I'd put you over my knee and give you such a good tanning, you couldn't sit down for a month."

Jill replied, "You and who else, Mister Asch? I'm not afraid of men who lost their spines years ago."

Asch's face stiffened at the remark.

Then he called Jill a name.

Jerry angrily said, "You apologize to her!"

Asch looked his way and then gave him a certain gesture. Jerry was a little shocked by it. He had seen folks give the gesture in New York City, but he didn't think anyone used it this far out west.

Just then, the door swung open and Ches Kinderstrom entered, looking at both of them questioningly.

"Is anything the matter?" he asked.

"Yes!" said Jill. "Your damn newspaper is calling for an 'extermination' of the rustler problem."

Kinderstrom's eyes came alive and he smirked at her. "So?"

"You don't mean rustlers," she said, looking at him levelly. "You mean homesteaders. Meaning *us*. People like me and my brother."

Jerry hated to interrupt her, but he felt he had to be heard too.

"And what about this headline? 'George Bingham killed resisting arrest.'"

Kinderstrom said irritably, "If you don't stop waving that newspaper in my face, I will break your hand."

Jerry threw aside the newspaper and said, "Did you write that article?"

"Every word," said Kinderstrom.

"Then you're a liar!"

Kinderstrom's eyes burned into Jerry's. He wasn't used to folks calling him a liar to his face, certainly not in Europe where he had lied and cheated for years.

Asch said, "You see, Mister Kinderstrom?   Two trouble-makers."

Kinderstrom took Jerry by the arm and said, "Tom, if you'll assist me."

Asch came through the wooden gate and said enthusiastically, "*Yes, sir*, Mister Kinderstrom!" He swung around the counter and grabbed Jill's arm.

However, he gripped it so tightly, she cried out in pain. Forgetting that his own arm was in Kinderstrom's grip, Jerry started to move towards them.

He shouted, "You let go of her!"

Jerry raised his fist towards Asch, but before he could follow through, Jill hauled off and punched the typesetter in the jaw. Asch fell back over the wooden gate and crashed into a large tray filled with set type for that day's headline. It all spilled onto the ink-stained floor practically on top of him. His visor and spectacles had fallen off and he looked up at Jill with some fear.

"What's the matter, Mister Asch?" she asked defiantly. "Why aren't you putting me over your knee for a tanning?"

Releasing Jerry, Kinderstrom reached out and spun Jill around to face him. Then he slapped her so hard, she fell back against the counter and slid to the floor.

With Kinderstrom's back to him, Jerry angrily grabbed the Swede around the neck and put him in a headlock. Kinderstrom tried to pull Jerry's arm off, but the New Yorker was too strong. After all, getting into physical combat was not something he did very often, despite his threat to break Jerry's hand.

With his free arm around Jerry waist, Kinderstrom pulled him backwards. The two men struggled for a few moments and, in this bizarre dance, moved uncomfortably close to the front window.

Jill sat up on the ground and felt her right cheek, which was now colored an ugly crimson. She watched helplessly as the two men suddenly lunged forward and crashed through the window, with Kinderstrom's back taking the full impact as they fell out onto the sidewalk.

Staring at the scene, she said, "Jesus!"

Out on the street, passersby stopped and watched, soon forming a crowd around the two combatants and cheerfully rooting for either one or the other. Meanwhile, Phil Devery and another McDermott ranch hand named Jess Reid, had just left the Quarter Moon Saloon directly across the street from the newspaper office. They were heading back to their horses for a ride back to McDermott's spread when the fight caught their attention. They both stood back and watched it with interest.

"Well, well," said Devery, with some amusement. "Look at our Swedish paper-pusher. Didn't know the square-0head was such a wildcat."

As Reid's eyes took in the scene, he asked, "Should I buy in?"

"No, not yet. Let's see how little Stockholm handles this dude."

Their hats had rolled off somewhere and their fine jackets were now ripped into shabby rags by glass shards. Still wrapped around each other, the two men awkwardly rose and Kinderstrom tried to push Jerry's head back by clawing his face. At that point, the New Yorker was grateful that his opponent had immaculately clean hands and tastefully trimmed fingernails.

Since the two men were so close to each other, Jerry had no room to swing his arm for a good punch. Instead, he did the only thing he could do in such close quarters; he lifted his knee and plowed it into Kinderstrom's crotch.

The Swede opened his mouth in pain and took his hand off Jerry's face. Jerry blinked as his eyes adjusted to the daylight. Then, grabbing a handful of Kinderstrom's torn coat in his fist, he reached back with his other hand and followed through with a hard punch to the Swede's finely chiseled nose. Kinderstrom cried out and fell back into the street in a cloud of dust.

Right after the punch, Devery said quietly, "*Now* you buy in."

Reid ran across the street and came upon Jerry just as he was turning around.

Jill saw him coming and cried, "Look out!"

But it was too late. Reid spun Jerry around and hit him in the face. The blow made Jerry's head spin and he was totally caught off-guard when Reid crowded into him and flattened him against the building's outer wall. Jerry's back struck the brick surface painfully, and he winced when he got a whiff of Reid's bad breath in his nostrils.

Pinning the other man against the wall, Reid brought up his elbow and struck Jerry across the face with it. At that point, the pinned man saw stars and tried to shake his head to clear his vision.

Grinning wickedly, Reid put his arm across Jerry's neck, choking him. Jerry had been pushing back against the other man, but Reid was heavier and an experienced brawler to boot, and he easily shrugged off Jerry's efforts to break free.

Enjoying his opponent's helplessness, Reid slid his free hand down to his holster and rested his fingers on the ivory-handled gun butt. Then he started to lift the gun free.

Being so close to him, Jerry instantly felt the move and knew what Reid was doing. Soon, the gun cleared leather and Jerry, with his left hand, tried to stop him from lifting the gun any further, but Reid's strength was incredible. Helplessly, he felt Reid start to turn the gun barrel towards his stomach.

Desperately, Jerry inserted his fingers under his torn coat and tried to reach the shoulder holster. Sweat was blinding him and Reid's elbow on his throat was sapping his breath.

Straining, he finally got one finger curled around the trigger of the double-action Colt. With the tip of Reid's gun finally aimed at Jerry's stomach, the gunman was about to pull the trigger until he heard the shot between them and felt a flaming heat sear his chest. Crying out, he leaped away from Jerry and dropped his gun as he saw the other man's coat catch fire.

Jerry quickly freed the Colt and pointed it at Reid, its barrel still smoking. Then, he took the tattered coat with his free hand and ripped and tore until the burning garment was completely off his body. Breathing hard, he tossed the still-smoldering rags into the street.

"Too bad," he said tiredly. "I always liked that coat."

Then he stared at Reid and tried to relax, but it was hard. This man had tried to kill him, something he had never experienced back in midtown Manhattan.

Reid just stood there and glared at him defiantly, his gun on the ground and his fallen Stetson lying next to it.

"You got the upper hand now, don't you, dude?"

Jerry didn't answer him; he just took a few steps closer and stood in front of him.

The crowd surrounding them didn't breathe; they just watched intently. Standing near them, Jill stared at Jerry uncertainly.

Reid grinned at him and said, "Soft livin' back east is all you know, pretty boy. You ain't got the guts to shoot me."

Jerry said quietly, "You're right."

He swung the .45 and the heavy iron barrel crashed against Reid's skull. The gunman's head exploded in pain as he sank to the ground.

Jerry looked down at the fallen man and saw his blood mix with the dirt of the street. He had never hit a man over the head with a pistol before, but he had seen an Irish cop knock out some armed ruffian in Hell's Kitchen one night and had idly wondered what it felt like. Having now done the act himself against another kind of ruffian, he had to admit it felt good.

Watching the scene, Devery was surprised that Reid had lost the fight. Quickly, he stepped forward and his hand went to his holstered gun. Jerry still held the pistol out in the open, so he figured he could claim he killed him in self-defense. Confidently, Devery drew his gun and aimed as he moved forward.

That's when Jill stuck her foot out and tripped him. Devery fell face-down in the street and his gun tumbled to the ground far out of his reach. Quickly, Jill stepped forward and her boot stepped on his outstretched hand. The gunman cried out as she ground the heel into his fingers.

Bitterly, she said, "You won't be shooting any folks for a while, I reckon."

Suddenly a gunshot behind Jill made her stop her grinding.

Jerry lowered the gun when he saw the marshal with his smoking pistol aimed at the sky.

Glaring at them, Rawlins shouted, "Now what the hell is going on around here?"

Still dusting himself off, his clothes now in rags, Ches Kinderstrom cut a ridiculous figure; and if he was too pompous to notice it, the crowd that stared at him sure did. They had to stifle their laughter as he rose from the street and approached Rawlins.

"Marshal," he said, catching his breath, "that man and woman attacked me and Tom Asch in the newspaper office. Then Mister Devery and Mister Reid came to our assistance."

People in the crowd shouted him down with "No!" and "He's a liar!"

One man in overalls said, "What that boy in rags says ain't true, Marshal. That big fella lyin' on the ground with his head bleedin' tried to kill the dude."

"One way or the other," said Rawlins, scanning the crowd of onlookers, "I'll get the real story. But right now, Miss Carmody, I'd like you to do me one special favor."

Jill said cheerfully, "Sure, Marshal, what is it?"

"Get your damn boot heel off Phil Devery's fingers!"

CHAPTER THREE

THE ALCOHOL-SOAKED CLOTH STUNG HIM, AND HIS BACK RECOILED when it made contact.

"Oww! That hurts!"

"'Sposed to," said Dr. Griffin. "It's gotta burn you a little so it can clean out the cuts."

Jerry felt pain and discomfort as he sat with his shirt off in Griffin's office. The stuff he was being dabbed with might as well be acid. He was especially ill at ease with Jill seated on a stool a few feet away watching him.

She said gently, "I forgot to thank you for stepping in."

Jerry looked at her and said drily, "Twern't nothin', ma'am."

She smiled at him. Then she shook her head and said, "I can't believe a dude could do some of the things I saw you do out in that street."

Jerry asked sincerely, "Why? Just 'cause I'm from the east, I'm not supposed to able to defend myself?"

Jill looked down and blushed, something that attracted Jerry further.

"Well," she explained lamely, "I don't mean that..."

He grinned and said, "I think I know what you mean. That's certainly the first storefront window I've ever crashed through."

Doc Griffin said, "Well, just make sure it's your last." For emphasis, he pressed the cloth harder on the back of Jerry's neck.

"Oww! You did that on purpose."

"Can't help it," said Griffin, deadpan, "I love my job."

"I bet."

"Let's just say that you're very lucky the other fella's back took the brunt of the impact when you both went through. Otherwise those glass shards would've cut your face to ribbons."

"You know," Jerry mused, "some store windows in New York are now made of reinforced glass."

"Reinforced glass," said Griffin, pausing, "what's that?"

"It's a special kind of glass they put metal wire through to make it less breakable."

"Glass with metal wire in it? Is that a fact?"

Jerry nodded. "Um-hm. We have a lot of...oh, hooligans in New York who like breaking display windows in jewelry stores. Hell's Kitchen alone has enough of them to fill one of your jails."

"My goodness," said Griffin. "Seems the east isn't the cradle of civilization we all thought it was. Right, Jill?"

Jill nodded absently. She wasn't listening to their talk; she was staring at Jerry's well-muscled chest. *Not bad for a paper-pushing attorney*, she thought. Jerry caught her watching him and wanted to turn aside, but Griffin ordered, "Be still! You'll make me spill this good whiskey."

"Sorry."

"That's all right. Stay still now..." He went over to a cabinet, put down the cloth and returned with a pair of tweezers. "Easy does it now..." He put the tweezers on Jerry's shoulder and pulled out a sliver of glass. "Ahh! Got it! The last piece. You may dress now, young man."

Jerry rose gratefully and went over to a coat hook for his shirt and coat, though Jill was disappointed to see him put them on. As he buttoned his shirt, he said, "Thanks for running over to the hotel and getting me a clean shirt and coat. I don't think folks in town would appreciate my walking through the streets half-naked."

She said, more or less to herself, "I've got no problem with it."

"What?"

"Nothing...What will you do now?"

Jerry shrugged into his coat and reached for his derby on the roll-top desk.

"I'm going to find out how my father died, since Rawlins didn't seem to have any information he could give me."

"Believe me," she said, "he knows. He's just protecting his bosses."

"It would seem so. When Kinderstrom threatened to kill me, instead of jailing him, Rawlins just said, 'Well, folks say things in the heat of the moment they don't really mean.' Oh please!"

He saw Jill smiling at his poor imitation of Rawlins.

"Did I sound good?"

"A little too much Manhattan in your drawl."

"I'll try better next time." He turned to Griffin and asked, "How much would it be, Doc?"

Griffin waved him away and said, "On the house, son. Anyone who buffaloes one of McDermott's trash the way you did, deserves a medal."

Jerry said, "Well, thanks." Then he turned to Jill and looked at her oddly. *"Buffaloed?"*

Grinning, she took his arm and led him from the office.

"You have a lot to learn about the west, Mister Bingham..."

Reid's head was still pounding despite the bandage wrapped

around it. At least he was seated on a plush couch; unfortunately, it was in Len Cagle's office. Cagle himself was seated behind his desk, shaking his head.

"I thought you boys were tough," he said curtly.

Devery stood near the door with his hat in his hand. He looked at the floor briefly. Then, as he went to his shirt pocket for the makings, he felt the stab of pain in his fingers and winced.

That damn bitch, he thought. I'll get her for this, I swear!

Cagle stared at both of them coldly. Then he said, "Mister McDermott is at the Cattlemens' House right now. Therefore, he's authorized me to give you both your time."

Devery swallowed and asked, "Mister McDermott *knows* about what happened already?"

"*The whole town* knows about how you two were made into fools."

Both men started to protest, but Cagle held up a firm hand and silenced them.

"Listen!" he said, raising his voice. "Fear is *everything* in our business. The public *has* to be afraid of us in order for us to succeed in our plans, is that understood?"

Devery and Reid just looked at each other in confusion. Then they faced Cagle and nodded enthusiastically, as if they understood him completely.

Cagle was not fooled.

Patiently, he said, "If two men can't handle some fancy Dan from the east, as well as a *girl*, well, we can't have those men working for Tad McDermott."

"But, Mister Cagle," said Devery, "we can fix that. Give us another chance and we'll take care of 'em."

Cagle pounded his fist on the desk and glared at them.

He said, "During the fight, Mister Kinderstrom saw you two leaving the Quarter Moon. You were both right across the street.

You could have run across and taken care of Bingham as soon as you saw the fight. Lord knows, Rawlins would've called it self-defense. But no! You both stood there and let Mister Kinderstrom get beaten up before you took a hand."

"Seems that way, don't it?"

"It *was* that way, Mister Devery!" Veins started popping in Cagle's neck as he stared at them.

Devery began awkwardly, "It's just that...Well, I guess we just wanted to teach that Kinderson a little lesson."

"First of all," Cagle said irritably, "it's Kinder*strom*! Second, it's not for you two to decide who gets a, as you say, 'lesson' in this outfit. That privilege belongs to Tad McDermott, now is that clear?"

The two cowboys said nothing. Devery just looked at the floor; Reid just felt his throbbing skull.

Finally, Reid said, "We're both real sorry, Mister Cagle."

Cagle looked at them and said nothing for a while. The two men looked at each other, not knowing what to make of his silence.

Finally, after a few moments, he asked, "Do you really want to make up for this?"

Both of them nodded vigorously.

"Quinn and Hardy took some men out on another run. Wait till they return. I'll let Charlie decide about you."

They both grinned and thanked Cagle profusely. Then they left.

Cagle sat quietly for a moment. Then he opened his desk drawer and removed a ledger. He went through it quickly, finally stopping on a certain page with a list of names on it. He took out his pen, put it to the list and then struck a line through two names.

Lucas Tenney couldn't believe his wife sometimes. She had

awakened him from a deep sleep to say that someone was in their toolshed. He got up groggily, threw on his trousers over his long drawers and, in his bare feet, hobbled out to the shed to where he kept his horse-plow and his tools. The place was six feet by seven, and musty inside, with sunlight filtering in through the spaces between its thin wooden walls. For what possible reason would anyone have to break into the shed? To steal his old plow? His hammer and nails and rusty old handsaw? He'd wondered if May had been sweeping the floors too hard or got too much sun while working the fields right along with him.

Lucas hobbled over to the barn to hitch up the buckboard. He dreaded the long ride; the road was bumpy, and it played havoc with his lower back muscles, but they needed supplies. Perhaps Tommy could ride with him today. The boy needed to see something else besides this Godforsaken countryside.

Tenney looked up and his eyes scanned the clouds. *Looks like a storm coming.* He wondered if he should get his and Tommy's rain slickers, but the noises in the distance made him look west, beyond the corral. The earth was shaking beneath his feet. Horses were approaching, a good many of them.

He glanced back at the house. May and Tommy were inside having lunch. He wondered whether he should get the Winchester hung on the wall just inside the door. He paused, not sure of what to do.

In moments, the riders came up to the property and stopped just outside their fence.

Lord, thought Tenney, there must be a dozen of them!

Fearfully, he took two steps back and watched them. They were just sitting their horses and staring at him as if he were something strange to them. Their silence unnerved him.

Then, he saw one of the cowboys, a surly-looking gent with a black mustache, nod his head to the man next to him. Out came a lasso and in seconds the man had looped the rope around a fence post. After seeing this, other cowboys removed ropes from saddles and also cast their lassos over other posts. Then, turning their horses around, they kicked their mounts forward and the fence all around the property bent and strained and finally uprooted from the ground with a loud splintering of wood.

Tenney ran towards the house, but a gunshot sounded, and a bullet pierced his kneecap just above the joint. He screamed and fell just before his front door. Alerted by the noise, May and Tommy came outside.

"Lucas!" his wife screamed.

Tommy started to turn back to the front door and the Winchester, but Charlie Quinn pointed his gun and shouted, "Hold it!"

The boy heard the command and suddenly stopped.

"Make another move and we kill your pa."

Tommy froze in fear. He didn't know what was going on, except that they had shot his pa.

"What do you want?" May screamed at them.

None of the riders answered her. Instead, one of the lead riders dismounted and calmly walked towards the shed, pausing to step over the broken fence posts lying on the ground before him. Standing in front of the shed, he kicked the door open and looked inside. Then he turned back and signaled to Quinn.

"Bring them," Quinn ordered.

Several riders dismounted and walked over to the family. May screamed at them and tried to raise her fists, but one of the men slapped her hard in the face. Tommy tried to attack the man, but Al Hardy grabbed him by the hair and yanked his head back hard. In his other hand was a Colt, which he pushed against the boy's skull; its iron-cold barrel and sight slamming into his temple.

"Don't make a move," he hissed at him, "or I'll kill your folks for sure. You hear me, boy?"

Tommy had tears in his eyes, frightened for himself and his parents. He nodded.

"Good!"

Quinn dismounted and walked over to the shed. He gestured to the riders in front of the cabin and they roughly pulled the family across the front yard towards the shed. Lucas Tenney shouted in pain when the two cowboys on either side of him pulled him over, his legs dragging behind him. A pool of blood quickly spread across the yard as they dragged him.

"No!" screamed May. She tried to break away from the two cowboys who held her and reached out to Lucas, but Charlie Quinn lifted his boot heel and kicked her in the small of her back. She screamed in pain and sagged to the ground. Tommy tried to interfere, but there were too many of them crowding him and holding onto his arms and legs as they dragged him. With her back in searing pain, May was now being dragged in the dirt along with her husband.

The riders stopped before the shed.

Lucas weakly asked, "Who are you?"

Instead of answering him, Quinn nodded, and Hardy went into the shed. A moment later he came out and held up a cow hide that had recently been sheared off.

"You were right, Charlie," he said. "This must be the rustlers' hideout." He tried to stop himself from laughing as he said it.

Lucas said, "Rustlers!"

May shouted, "You men must be insane!"

Quinn stared at her with no expression.

Hardy grinned and said, "What do you think, Charlie? Think we should be put in the bughouse?"

Quinn didn't answer.

Instead, he just drew his gun and shot May in the head. Her head recoiled and the surprised cowboys who held her let her body fall to the ground. The others knew that May would be killed anyway; they just didn't figure it would be done so soon.

Tommy screamed and Lucas shut his eyes tightly, tears already forming in them.

Amidst all the noise, Quinn said nothing; he seemed to be lost for a moment, as if he was somewhere else.

Hardy said, "Charlie?"

When he saw that Quinn wouldn't answer, Hardy said the others, "Throw 'em in the shed."

Both man and boy wailed loudly, but the cowboys holding onto them ignored their agony and pulled their captives in through the doorway of the shed. Already weakened from loss of blood, Lucas was thrown roughly onto the dirt floor, the impact making his plow handle tip forward and fall to the ground noisily.

However, when they picked up Tommy and tried to push him through the doorway, the boy grabbed hold of it with both hands, stubbornly struggling against the cowboys' efforts to heave him inside. The two men tried to pry his fingers loose, pounding them with their fists as Tommy screamed.

Finally, one cowboy said to the other, "Use the butt of your gun on his fingers."

"Got a better idea," Hardy said.

He drew his gun, aimed it at Tommy's back and fired. The boy dropped to the ground and the two cowboys then lifted his body and threw it in on top of his father.

Hardy indicated May's body and said, "Her too."

Two other riders bent over and picked up the body, then dragged it over to the shed and threw it inside, next to the others.

"My God!" screamed Lucas. "What're you going to do?!"

The men didn't answer. They just slammed the door shut and bolted it.

Hardy said, "Get some brush and put it around the shed."

One of the men asked, "You gonna *roast* them too?"

Hardy stared at him and said, "Witnesses, Cal. *Witnesses*! Do you want to hang?"

The man obediently followed the others and started to gather brush as well as the fallen fence posts.

Hardy walked over to Quinn.

He quietly asked, "You seein' *her* again?"

Quinn took a deep breath and answered, "For a spell. Felt like I wasn't even here."

"You looked like you were miles away."

Quinn looked at him with no expression and said, "Maybe I was, Al. Maybe I was..."

"Yeah."

"So, what's the fee now?"

"Fifty for the man. Twenty-five apiece for the woman and boy."

"Nice piece of change for an afternoon's work."

Then they both heard the crackling flames and turned around.

The shed was on fire. Soon, the walls disappeared in sheets of flame and, as the minutes passed, they rose higher and consumed the tin roof. It collapsed within the four burning walls in a sudden splintering of burning wood and ash. Black smoke rose in the sky in ugly clouds.

The riders stood back and watched as the fire cast twisted shadows on them.

Quinn and Hardy watched also, their eyes riveted to the sight.

Then, vaguely, from somewhere inside the inferno, they all heard a dying man's scream.

They had traveled miles from town, way out on the flatlands that spread across the valley with the North Platte to the south and the Sand Hills to the north. Then they crossed Pawnee Creek at a shallow bend and made for the low foothills. The foliage was dense here, and the two skirted the trees by carefully walking their horses down some narrow trails that Jill had known about for years.

Jerry asked, "Is this the only way for you to get to town?"

"No," she said. "It's just kind of a shortcut."

He leaned forward in the saddle to duck under a low-hanging branch.

"It may be short, but it's kind of inconvenient."

He had rented his horse from the local hostler and was pleasantly surprised to see how easy he was adjusting to being in the saddle. In New York, his prime transportation had been the subways or, if traveling shorter distances, a hansom driven by some man in a fancy top hat and cloak who usually frequented Fifth Avenue.

Jill said, "It may be inconvenient, but these trees prevent McDermott's boys from coming at us all at once."

Jerry ducked his head again and said, "McDermott's boys?"

"You really are new here, aren't you, Jerry? Hasn't your father ever mentioned them?"

He shoved a branch away from his eyes and said quietly, "We hadn't spoken in many years."

She swept her hair out of her eyes and stared at him.

"Oh."

"Yeah, 'oh'."

"I'm sorry. I didn't want to bring up...well, I won't mention it anymore."

Jerry held onto his derby as another branch swept by.

"No," he said, "it's all right. It's just that..." He looked down at the pommel and paused. He had not really had time to shed any tears about the old man, and he worked hard to fight them back now.

Finally, he said, "When I was a kid, I used to look up to him. He was my hero. The folks on the west side loved him. They called him a crusader because he tried to make sure their voices were heard. He was concerned about the slums, the substandard food they sold in the stores, the lack of sanitation. He wanted to give factory workers their rights, because, let's face it, they still don't have any."

Jill raised her arm and held back a tree branch as she passed under it, but her eyes were watching him intently.

He continued, "My mother had died of fever some years ago; the filthy apartment building we were living in certainly contributed to her death, I'm sure...Anyway, my father ran for alderman in the Fourteenth Ward three times, but he lost every time. He wouldn't play along with Tammany Hall, and, rather spitefully I thought, they made sure he couldn't be elected dog catcher." He swayed to his right and avoided another branch, then righted himself. "I was just starting out as a lawyer. I didn't go to law school or anything like that, there was no money. Instead, I studied his law books and memorized everything. I figured that when I knew enough, I was going to be just like him, clean as a whistle. Pretty soon, I got a job with a law firm in midtown Manhattan, right on Fifth Avenue. He was so proud of me then."

Jerry's eyes went to the pommel again; he took a breath.

"Then one day, I came home from the office and found him in the living room with some fancy-Dan in a Prince Albert coat and a Homburg. Just as I was entering the room, they both got up and Dad was stuffing an envelope into his breast pocket—but not soon enough that a hundred-dollar bill didn't float its way to the floor right at his feet. Before he got a chance, I stooped over and picked it up. There it was in my hand, a hundred bucks. More money than either of us had seen at any one time. I stared at both of them with tears in my eyes. Dad looked like he wanted to be anywhere but in that room. And the sport in the fancy duds just looked at me oddly, as if what they were doing was perfectly normal. Tammany knew that Dad had the respect of the community and it seems that they wanted his blessing on the building of a 'social club' somewhere in the neighborhood. I could only take a good guess who the members of this club would be. Their plan sounded fine—only they'd have to evict ninety-six families and knock down two apartment buildings in order to build this trophy to Tammany's ego."

When he paused, Jill quietly asked, "So you split with him then?"

"Boy, did I! I asked the other tenants about this fancy-looking fellow and it seems he'd been up in our place quite a few times." He shook his head sadly and said, "I wondered where Dad suddenly got the money to get me better suits than the hand-me downs I was wearing.

"I moved out after that. In the meantime, the big boys rewarded him for his loyalty by throwing him to the wolves when the reformers came to call. Dad had to leave town with a grand jury nipping at his heels. Looking back on it, I guess he couldn't turn state's evidence. Tammany would've sent a couple of its hooligans over and dad would soon find himself tumbling down a flight of stairs in our building." He added bitterly, "An 'accidental death', as Tammany's crooked cops would call it."

Jill looked at him oddly and said, "*Cops?*"

Jerry gave her a little smile and then faced the trail.

"You've got a lot to learn about the East, Miss Carmody."

"I guess I do. So, your father came here?"

Jerry nodded. "I didn't hear from him in years until a friend passing through the Midwest brought back a newspaper mentioning him as an attorney in the employ of the big cattle outfits." He shook his head again. "It seems there's a Tammany Hall everywhere, isn't there?"

They made it through the toughest part of the undergrowth; there were fewer trees here and soon the two of them could sit erect in their saddles without fear of being knocked off.

Then, to his surprise, Jill reached over and squeezed his hand.

"But you don't know the whole story," she said.

Jerry looked at her; he was not only moved by the gesture, but he liked the touch of her hand on his. There was no doubt that the palm and fingers had taken on the toughness that can only come with hard ranch work, but he also felt the softness beneath the persistent calluses. He had a feeling that this woman didn't perform this gesture with just any man.

Jill looked into his eyes and said, "He changed, Jerry. He really did."

"I wish I could believe that."

"Believe it. For the past year, your father has been fighting for the homesteaders. He used to work for the cattlemen, but he got sick of it. They only started murdering the homesteaders in the past year when Tad McDermott became head of the Combine. He hired a band of killers and sends them out to terrorize anyone the cattlemen claim is on *their* range. McDermott's boys are a pack of animals; women, children, they don't care who they kill. You got a taste of their brutality back in town."

Jerry stared at her.

"You mean those two men? The one who I struck over the head—"

"*Buffaloed.*"

He cleared his throat and continued, "Buffaloed. You mean these men were part of that group?"

She nodded grimly.

"Jesus. I thought they were just two drunken cowboys looking for a fight."

"The McDermott crew isn't looking for fights, they're looking to *take lives*! And to them, the more the merrier." Jill squeezed his hand again. He saw the sparkle in her hazel eyes when she said gently, "Your father couldn't stomach murder. He drew the line there. He told us about when he quit McDermott; he said they had a terrible row." She smiled thinking about it. "He was too much of a gentleman to mention what curse words they used, and he kept substituting words like 'gosh-darn idiot' and 'mucking moron'."

"You met him?"

"He's met a *lot* of the homesteaders. He said he had to know the people he was fighting for. He tried to get us to fight McDermott through legal channels, but you can see how that's been working out..."

Jerry didn't say anything for a while. He blinked his eyes rapidly, and felt tears starting to form. Seeing this, Jill looked away and casually said, "Better keep our eyes ahead. Another branch could pop out and decapitate both of us."

Jerry looked at her as she rode ahead of him. She knew the right thing to say and just how to say it. He had always liked a smart woman, and this one made all the fancy dressed women back in New York look positively feeble-minded. Maybe Jill didn't know which side of a plate the silverware went, but there was something else about her that was a lot more valuable.

They soon came out onto a clearing that slanted down into a low hill. A log cabin was at the bottom of it.

That's when they heard the gunshot.

Jerry sat frozen in his saddle.

"What's that?"

Jill wryly said, "Jesse James."

"What?"

"Just my brother performing his circus act."

Jerry looked at her oddly as they both walked their horses down the hill. After they dismounted and tied their horses to the hitching rail in front, they went around to the back and found Morgan in the act of cocking his .45 and aiming at a bottle perched on a rock.

He fired and Jerry tried not to jump in his shoes. A bottle splattered into fragments.

"Morg," said Jill.

He turned around, surprised to see Jerry. He quickly holstered his gun.

"This is Jerry Bingham. Jerry, my brother Morg."

At first, Morgan gave a polite smile as they shook hands, but then his smile dropped when he looked at him.

"Bingham?"

"Right."

"Oh," Morgan said soberly, "I'm so sorry."

Strong grip. "Thank you," Jerry said, trying not to think of his hand.

Jill said, "I went to the Sentinel complaining about another one of their headlines and Tom Asch and that damn Swede who runs it tried to throw me out. Jerry stood up for me."

Morgan smiled at him and said, "Is that a fact?"

"Yep. He even went through the window of the newspaper office for me."

"Really? Well, Jill doesn't get too many men going through storefront windows for her." Then he gave Jill a knowing look, not saying anything further. She knew what that look meant. She could almost hear him adding, *In fact, she doesn't get too many men, period!*

"Come on inside," she said. "I'm sure I can fix something."

Perhaps it was the sound of the wind swaying some tree branches behind him, but the noise made Jerry glance back and he suddenly noticed the lone tree stump which sat amidst a grove of full, lush cottonwoods. He paused and wondered why only one tree had been cut down.

Jerry indicated the stump and said, "That's odd."

"What?" asked Morgan.

Jill saw the stump and a tension grew within her.

"That lone stump," he answered. "It kind of sticks out like a sore thu—"

Morgan said icily, "Listen, Mister, I don't tell you what to do in *your* backyard."

Jerry stared at him and quietly said, "I'm sorry."

Morgan calmed down then; in fact, he almost seemed emotionally drained. "Let's get inside," he said, and sullenly walked away.

Trying to change the subject, Jill forced a smile and said, "I make the greatest apple pies. I promise you you won't leave here hungry." Then she turned and followed her brother to the front of the house.

Jerry lingered in the yard, taking just a moment longer to look back at the tree stump. Then he shook his head and followed the others.

CHAPTER FOUR

"No wonder he was upset when I asked about the tree-stump."

They were both atop one of the low hills which dotted the area. A light wind blew the high grass which grew in thatches among the rocks, and Jill pushed back the hair which was covering her face. She was studying him carefully, measuring how he would react to another one of her brother's peculiarities.

All through the meal, as Jerry gratefully ate Jill's homemade pie, Morgan seemed constantly distracted, as if this respite from target-shooting was an unnecessary obligation he had to perform to please his sister. Jill tried to smile and inject some much-needed cheer at the table, but Morgan kept poking at the slice of pie with his fork and barely attempting to eat it. He smiled a little; forced smiles that did nothing to hide the sadness in his eyes. He tried to make idle banter, but Jerry could see that the man's heart wasn't in it. Shoving away the plate with the half-eaten pie, Morgan rose and said he was going into town for supplies. Jill was glad he was at least going out. She was brought down by his manner; and his leaving also proved to her that at least he had no problem leaving her alone with Jerry, whom he apparently trusted.

Jerry was still gazing down at the cabin when he said, "That poor man. Finding his wife like that..." He shook his head. "No man should have to endure that."

"Many in the valley still do."

He looked at her then and instantly saw the bitterness on her face. This time she didn't sweep the hair from her face as the wind again blew it in her eyes. Jerry identified with her anger, but as he stood there gazing at her with her hair across her eyes and her face lit just right by the mid-afternoon sun, he was vaguely aware that he was starting to feel something else about her.

He quickly turned away from her and walked over to the edge, gazing down at the wide expanse of land beneath him. It was breathtakingly beautiful, as he believed most of the west was. He couldn't conceive of men being such barbarians that they'd murder each other over it with such mindless abandon.

Jill asked, "Something wrong?"

Jerry paused. Then he said, "It's just what some folks would do to get some land." He looked back at her. "If the cattlemen lynched Morgan's wife, why didn't they take this property? You know, just move right in, knock down the cabin, put up their own fences."

Jill came up to him and said evenly, "Because I decided that my brother shouldn't be alone. So, I moved out of my father's house and came here to live with him. My father was angry about that. He had never considered Morgan *his* son because he was the son of his second wife and, let's face it, Morgan was a rebellious boy and couldn't stand my father anyway. One night, Morg got so mad at him, he accused him of murdering his mother."

"And what do you think?"

Jill shook her head as she gazed across the valley.

"I don't know. I knew that my father has a cruelty in him, especially towards women, but when Morg told me that Dad was part of a group that murdered his wife, I was through with him forever..." She faced Jerry and he saw sadness in her eyes. "But to Dad, I guess he still considers me his little girl. To answer your question, *that's* the reason McDermott's crew hasn't bothered with us since Morg's wife was hanged. It's *me*, Jerry. They won't attack this place while I'm here. And I know that the minute I leave, they'll come and string up my brother the way they did Emmy Lou. I can't ever leave here. I can't ever be with..."

She looked away then.

Jerry finished the sentence for her. "You can't ever be with a man."

Embarrassed, she looked down and nodded.

Jill sniffed back a tear and said bitterly, "As God is my witness, I know that the moment it looks like some man is gonna take me away from here, the moment it looks like I'm no longer on this property and Morgan is all alone, my father will order McDermott's men to ride down here and murder him and burn this place to the ground."

Then she faced him again, her eyes red and her face crumpled in despair.

"And just when it looks like I found a man who—"

She stopped suddenly and Jerry was hoping desperately that she'd finish the sentence.

Then he saw that she was looking past him at the sky and he quickly turned around.

They both saw it plainly, the billowing black smoke several miles in the distance.

He muttered, "What the hell—"

"They're at it again!"

Jerry turned back to her and asked, "Where do you think they hit?"

Jill looked away for a moment and said, "I'm trying to remember. It's about ten miles away; who's out there now?" Then she looked sharply at him and said, "The Tenneys! I used to look after their little boy when they went up north to visit kin. Oh my God, Jerry!"

He asked quickly, "Does Morgan have a rifle?"

"Yes, but he broke the stock and it's being repaired in town. We'll take *mine*!"

Jerry nodded and followed her down the hill.

Soon they had mounted their horses and turned them in the direction of the burning cabin. Jill slid the rifle into the scabbard on her saddle and looked at Jerry as he sat his horse next to hers.

She smiled at him wryly and said, "All right, eastern man. You ready to ride like the devil was at your tail?"

Jerry replied, "I'll follow you anywhere."

Jill turned away and faced the trail again so Jerry wouldn't see her blush.

They rode hard through the open flatlands, closer and closer to the burning cabin. Downwind of the fire, Jerry's eyes were stinging, and his nostrils were filled with the odor of burning wood and ash as they neared the location.

They were topping a rise when they both stopped and looked down at the sight. The Tenneys' house was still intact, but it looked like the tool shed was a heap of still-burning wood and a charred tin roof. The walls had totally collapsed and the two had become vaguely aware of something else smoldering beneath it.

Jerry winced and said, "That awful smell!" Then he realized something else. "Oh my God!"

Jill was upset already, just looking down at the awful sight.

She was almost dreading what Jerry was going to say.

He said, "I remember a nine-alarm fire on West Forty-Fifth Street and Tenth Avenue some time last year. I was standing on the street behind the police lines and I smelled that same awful stench. The odor of burning flesh..."

She stared at him with fear in her eyes.

Then she yelled at her horse and spurred him down the incline. Shocked by the suddenness of her actions, Jerry anxiously followed her down the slope, trying to keep his horse from tripping over the fist-sized rocks and jutting crags along the way. When they reached the bottom, the odor was intense, and Jerry tried to ignore it as he followed her mount.

Then he saw something on the ground that looked like a small dog; it was slowly crawling in the dirt and was just inches from the path of Jill's horse. Yet she was so intent on getting to the house to see if everyone was all right, that she didn't see the figure.

Jerry shouted, "Jill!"

When her horse didn't stop, he quickly drew the double-action from his coat and fired one shot into the air.

Jill yanked on her reins and brought the horse to a sudden stop. Then, in a quick reflex movement, she drew the rifle from the scabbard and leveled it at Jerry.

He cried out, "Look behind you on the ground!"

Jill turned around and saw him then, his small bloodied arms spread out in the sand.

She muttered, "Oh, my God!"

Yanking her feet out of the stirrups, she dropped to the ground and bent down to the small figure. She turned his body over and held his head in her hand. Tommy's face was blackened by soot and dried blood was around the corners of his mouth.

"Damn it!" she said. "I rushed out and didn't bring any water!"

Jerry dismounted and started to pull his own canteen off the saddle.

Jill tried to keep lift the boy up, but when she put her other hand around his back to lift him up, he cried out in pain.

She quickly removed her hand and looked at it. Her fingers were covered with blood. She leaned over then and quickly saw the bleeding hole in his back.

Jerry crouched down beside her and handed her the open canteen.

Carefully, she put it to Tommy's parched lips and poured a trickle on them. The boy's tongue licked it gingerly and then he coughed.

Jerry's own throat was clogged with the stench of the burning wood nearby. He was wondering how Jill was able to take it without gagging. Quickly he took his derby off and fanned the air around them.

Then his eyes scanned the ground and he said, "A lot of riders were here."

Looking down at the boy in her arms, Jill stroked his hair and said, "And the fences have been pulled down. Take a good guess who did this..."

He tossed his hat aside and said, "Let's get him in the house."

She glanced at him and then looked down again at Tommy.

"We shouldn't move him."

"And we can't care for him in the shadow of a burning shed while he's lying in the dirt."

"All right," she said quietly. "But *careful*! Keep him off his back."

They lifted him up slowly, supporting him in such a way that his back wouldn't feel any further strain in the carrying. Yet the boy still cried out in pain, and their hearts went out to him as they quickly moved towards the house a few feet away.

"In a minute, son," he said. "We're almost there."

They carefully climbed the front steps and Jerry put his back to the screen door and pushed.

They passed the kitchen area and quickly skittered over to a bedroom, with Jill kicking the door in as they approached it. They didn't know whose bed was in the room, but looking at how big it was, Jerry guessed it had belonged to the boy's parents.

They laid him gently on his stomach, turning his head outwards so the pillow wouldn't smother him. Then they stood erect.

Jerry said, "I'll ride to town for a doctor."

Jill shook her head and said, "It's over thirty miles to town. There's no time!"

"I'm not going to stand here and watch this boy die!"

Jill anxiously ran her hand back through her hair and looked around anxiously. Then her attention focused on the kitchen. She quickly left the room and he heard her rummaging through the kitchen drawers and cabinets. In a few seconds, she returned with a bottle of whiskey and a small, but razor-sharp knife.

Jerry quickly grabbed her wrist.

"Are you crazy? You're not a doctor!"

Jill yanked her hand out of his grip and said, "What else can we do! The bullet's still in him and it's got to come out."

"And while you try, the boy could die of shock."

The boy coughed suddenly, and it pulled their attention back to him.

They both leaned over him. Jill dropped the knife on the mattress and put the bottle on the floor beside the bed. Then she picked up Tommy's hand, rubbing it gently to try to keep him warm.

Jerry put his hand on the boy's head and forced himself to smile. "Hey, little fella," he said, trying to sound amiable. "You're gonna be all right."

Tommy coughed to clear his throat. Then he said weakly, "Mister, you're a liar..."

Jerry glanced at Jill and saw the grim look on her face.

Tommy continued, "I may have a bullet in my back, but I ain't deaf. I heard ya'll talkin'."

Jerry swallowed the lump in his throat. Then he stroked the boy's head and said, "I'm sorry, son."

"How do ya'll think *I* feel?" Tears came to his eyes then as he tried to sit up.

Jill said gently, "Take it easy, Tommy. Preserve your strength."

 "They shot Ma and Pa!"

Jerry looked at him intently. "Who did, son?"

Jill bitterly said, "Who do you think?"

"Jill, please!" He turned back to the boy and asked gently, "Can you describe some of them to me?"

Jill said angrily, "Oh, Lord, Jerry! Leave him be!"

Jerry ignored her and asked gently, "Please, Tommy. What did they look like?"

Tommy's eyes shrunk back in his head and for a moment, the two of them thought that Tommy was fading, but then he said haltingly, "One had a black mustache and black eyes. Looked like a vulture. The other one had blond hair and a down-home accent, maybe Texas. There were...a whole mess of 'em.   Tore down our fences...threw Ma and Pa into the shed and fired it." Tears rolled down his cheeks and his breathing was getting labored. "There was...a trap door...near the floor at the back of the shed. Pa shoved me out just before the fire got 'em."

To her growing horror, Jill felt the boy's pulse becoming weaker.

Tommy winced in pain and said, "They called us...rustlers. Pa never stole a beef a day in his..."

They stared at him. With his hand on the boy's forehead, Jerry suddenly realized that his skin had become cold as ice.

Tommy's eyes closed, and the body relaxed suddenly.

Jill gaped at the little hand in hers and cried out, "Tommy. Tommy!"

She slowly released his hand and stood erect. Then, with an angry roar, she picked up the knife and threw it at the far wall. The blade embedded itself deeply in the wood; its bone handle quivering with the impact.

She suddenly turned to Jerry and buried her head in his chest. As he embraced her, he felt her tears through his shirt and her slim body in his arms as it rocked with sobs. Feeling the boy's death no less than she, he embraced her even tighter.

Then he peered over her shoulder and looked down at the boy lying peacefully on the bed. All pain and anguish were gone from him and he almost seemed to be asleep.

As he held her in his arms, Jerry's thoughts drifted, and it seemed as if he wasn't standing there at all, but instead, was watching everything from a great distance. Only one thing was on his mind then. He wondered what kind of people would commit a holy war against peaceful settlers and even murder their children for a plot of land. Gradually, he was realizing that nothing about the west was going to surprise him anymore...

They had ridden into town quietly, without fanfare or the need to call attention to themselves. They had not said a word to each other since they made the decision to ride to town after Tommy's death; they rode through the valley and twisted trails, past barbed wire fences and around vast herds of roving cattle, both lost in their own thoughts. They had both seen a child die, and both were helpless to prevent it. Jill rode with reddened eyes, and she blinked rapidly to hold back even more tears as she sullenly watched the trail. Jerry was still reeling from it all. He had detested the slum conditions in New York that brought filth and disease that killed children, but he had never been present when one of them had died.

Some people on the sidewalks recognized Jill and wondered why she was being so quiet about entering town this time, rather than galloping in as she always did to complain about something or other. She had her black Stetson on and pushed down low over her eyes, as if she didn't want anyone to see how emotionally-drained she was. Some folks recognized Jerry as the dude who stood up to two of McDermott's crew and wondered what he was doing there as well.

It wasn't long before they stopped in front of the Cattlemen's House.

After they dismounted and tied their horses to the tie rail, Jerry put his hand on her arm and said, "There's someone I have to see, but that can wait. You sure you don't want me to go with you?"

Jill shook her head sullenly. Then, without a word, she left him and went in through the front door. She had a time explaining to the fancy-dressed man who stood inside the door that she was Eugene Farnsworth's daughter and that she wanted to see him. He eyed her suspiciously, and after a few moments, had another fancy-dressed man usher her into the elevator. A young man in a uniform, named Kenneth looked at her, and when she inquired where Mr. Farnsworth was, he replied that he was in the fourth-floor lounge with his partners. Then he pulled the steel door closed and pushed the lever forward; then the lumbering elevator rose and slowly made its ascent to the fourth floor.

The servants stared at her as she passed them; she was still dressed in her range clothes, now dirty and blackened by ash from the fire, and they were in their crisp, neat uniforms. At first, she felt uncomfortable, but then she remembered why she was here, and it stiffened her backbone.

Jill walked into the club room and told still another fancy-dressed man that she was there to see Eugene Farnsworth. The man looked her up and down and made no attempt to hide it. It enraged her further and she was about to call him a choice name until he pointed out Farnsworth at the other end of the room. She proudly walked right past the costumed man whose head swiveled after her as she went by. Soon, she found herself before the five cattlemen who headed the Combine.

When she approached their circle of plush leather chairs, they all looked up in surprise; all except Tad McDermott, who knew who she was and openly glared at her.

Then, grinning at her maliciously, he said, "You're in the wrong place, little girl. The whorehouse is down the block."

Jill stared at him angrily and said, "You should know, Mister McDermott, since that's where your wife is."

McDermott's face became an angry mask and the knuckles of his hands turned milk-white as he tightly grasped the arms of his chair. No one was allowed to mention the wife he had cast aside, and for anyone in town to even whisper out loud what they all knew to be true meant a visit by one of McDermott's crew in the middle of the night; and as most folks knew all too well, McDermott's crew did not give warnings.

Farnsworth sat in the chair nearest to Jill when she entered. After her remark to McDermott, he leapt to his feet.

"Jill," he said harshly, "I don't know what you're doing here, but—"

Before he could finish, she gave him a stinging slap.

Shocked, Farnsworth stared at her and felt his reddened cheek.

Jill said bitterly, "That's for being a baby-murderer!"

All activity and talk in the entire room stopped and everyone stared at them.

Then she turned to all of them and screamed, "You're all baby-murderers!"

Farnsworth stared at his daughter with widened eyes and grabbed her arm, but she shook it out of his grip and faced him with such hatred, it made him swallow nervously.

She said, "I suppose you didn't know about the Tenneys, how you sent them out to murder the whole family, including Tommy. He was just a boy, but that didn't make any difference to those lunatics you employ. They shot him in the back and burned his folks alive!"

McDermott leaned forward and shouted, "We don't need some petticoat-wearin' rustler to tell us our job!"

Jill faced him then, fury rising within her. She took a few steps towards him, her fists balled at her sides. The others rose from their chairs, attempting to block her path, and Judge Alcott reached out and grabbed her arm, but she shook it loose and pushed her way past them.

Then Ridgeway stuck his foot out and she tripped and fell to the carpeted floor with a thud. Her Stetson rolled off and her hair fell before his eyes. The other partners stood over her and laughed, all except Farnsworth who stared at them angrily.

When Jill looked up, she saw McDermott already standing over her. From the floor, he looked like a giant, much taller than his six-foot-five-inch height.

Through his teeth, he said, "You need a tannin', girl." Then he swung his booted foot forward and kicked her in the pit of her stomach.

She doubled over in pain and groaned.

McDermott's gravelly voice hissed, "I wasn't even tryin' that time, girl. Now I'm gonna make sure no man'll have you." He swung his foot back again for another kick.

Farnsworth shouted, "Stop it! Stop it, Tad!"

McDermott's eyes went from her to the man shouting at him from a few feet away.

He hissed, "Maybe I should be doin' this to *you*. This bitch belongs to you and I've taken all that I can from her. But next time she comes anywhere near me, I will gouge out her eyes and break that long white neck of hers in five different places. You hear?"

Jill had her arms wrapped across her stomach tightly. She was coughing and some vomit was already staining the bright red carpet near McDermott's polished brown boots.

He said curtly, "Now get this whore outta here." Then he turned and walked out of the circle of chairs over to the bar at the far end of the room.

The other men standing over her just looked down at her for a moment, then walked away as well; none of them attempting to help her to her feet. Farnsworth was the last one and when he looked down at her, he saw the hateful eyes glaring up at him before he finally moved away to join the others.

Awkwardly, Jill picked up her hat and rose to her feet, trying not to wobble unsteadily as she did so. After she stood up, two servants came up and stopped before her.

She looked at both of them and said gravely, "That's all right. I think I could leave here without your help." She stumbled past them, one hand still on her stomach, and headed towards the stairs.

Jill donned her hat and then descended the staircase as carefully as she could without getting nauseous. Regardless of the pain she was still feeling, she was glad to have called them out, at least for Tommy's sake; but she wondered if her righteous outburst had not only put her in danger, but her brother as well.

Knowing Tad McDermott, she already knew the answer to that one.

CHAPTER FIVE

THE STARRETT CITY COURTHOUSE WAS A TWO-STORY BRICK building with a simple architectural plan. The courtroom was on the first floor and the city prosecutor's office and the offices of other local officials were on the second floor.

Jerry mounted the sleek stone steps to the second floor and went along the hallway. He stopped at a door marked William Connors, District Attorney and knocked.

He heard a voice say, "Come in."

After he entered and shut the door, Jerry took off his derby and looked around. He saw a man in his thirties with close-cropped dark brown hair, a well-tanned complexion and piercing brown eyes, seated at a desk and staring back at him. His coat was off, and the sleeves of his crisp white shirt were rolled up revealing tanned arms. To Jerry, it indicated that this man didn't spend all of his life indoors behind a desk. Still, there were some papers lying spread out before him and he looked like he was in the middle of writing on them. The no-nonsense look on his face told Jerry that he didn't like being interrupted.

"Yes?" The prompting sounded impatient.

"Mister Connors, my name is Jerry Bingham."

At first, it seemed the name didn't mean anything to him, but then the eyes became alert. Then he rose, went around his desk and held out his hand.

"Oh, Mister Bingham," he said, losing all his curtness, "I'm so sorry." They shook hands and Connors gestured for him to sit down. Jerry sat in a straight-back chair before the desk.

Connors said, "We all admired your father." Seeing the surprised look on Jerry's face, he asked, "You don't believe me?"

Jerry said levelly, "Well, frankly, Mister Connors, I was under the impression that this office stood with the cattlemen."

Connors sat back and paused, his eyes briefly scanning his desk blotter. Jerry figured he was weighing carefully what he was going to say.

"This town welcomes their business," said Connors evenly. "After all, they pump an awful lot of money into our economy."

Jerry looked at his own hands in his lap and he did a little pausing of his own. Then his eyes locked onto Connors' and he replied, "Perhaps, Mister Connors. Though from what I've seen of their methods, they don't act like ordinary businessmen, to say the least."

Cautiously, Connors asked, "You...don't like our cattlemen?"

Jerry's face became grim. He leaned forward and said bitterly, "No, Mister Connors, I don't like your cattlemen any more than I would any other child-murderer."

Connors raised his eyebrows and stared at him, though Jerry couldn't understand why. At first, he thought that Connors would put on an outraged pose and defend the cattlemen to the hilt. Instead, Connors rose from his chair, walked over to the door and opened it. He then peeked outside and looked both ways. Jerry didn't see anyone on the way up, and from the satisfied look on Connors' face, he assumed that no one was in the hallway now.

Connors closed the door and went to Jerry's chair. To his surprise, the man held out his hand.

Jerry looked at the proffered hand and said, "I don't understand, Mister Connors. Didn't we already do this?"

Connors grinned at him and said, "That was my handshake for a stranger, Mister Bingham. This one is for an ally."

Smiling, Jerry stood up and shook his hand for real this time.

A few minutes later, Connors was standing at his open window and looking down at the busy street below.

He said, "Look at them, Mister Bingham. Going to and fro, seeing to their businesses, seeing to their families' needs, celebrating Christmas and Easter and all the good Christian holidays in between. All of them so content with their station in life." He shook his head. "They've all been bitten by a rattlesnake and they're too stupid to know they've been filled with venom that's slowly killing them." He looked back at Jerry. "And from what you've told me you and the Carmody woman have found, the poison is getting worse all the time."

Jerry stood on the other side of the desk and studied him closely. When he entered Connors' office, he thought he would have a verbal fight on his hands, assuming that the D.A. would obstruct him at every turn. In some ways, however, what he found was much worse: a very bitter man.

Jerry said quietly, "Aren't you being a little too cynical? Not everyone is this town is waving McDermott's flag."

Connors looked at him, a wry smile on his face.

"I didn't think you folks from New York looked at the bright side of anything. I've heard so much about your own cynicism, and that you have good reason to for it. Your mounting crime statistics, your corrupt police officers, your crooked local government."

"Nothing lasts forever, Mister Connors. I used to work for a law firm consisting of graft-takers, but like all such enterprises, they were found out in time. You see, even corruption has to come to an end sometime."

Connors folded his arms and said, "Why, Mister Bingham, you surprise me. After all you've seen and been through, you still believe that there's something called goodness left in the world."

Jerry looked down and reddened at his hectoring tone.

Then he looked at him and answered plainly, "Yes, Mister Connors, I do."

Suddenly, Connors' face became serious and his tone was no longer playful.

He asked soberly, "Even when I tell you how your father died?"

Jerry stared back him grimly.

Then he asked, "How'd it happen? Mister Kinderstrom's newspaper just mentioned that he was the leader of a gang of cattle rustlers."

Connors said bitterly, "Autocrats like Mister Kinderstrom should go back to Europe and stay there with the other diehards of colonialism."

Jerry said curtly, "About my father, Mister Connors."

Connors sighed and looked down at the floor. Then he looked Jerry in the eye and said, "He was thrown off a cliff, Mister Bingham. Or at least that's the story I heard. Actually, McDermott's men said he 'resisted arrest' and accidentally fell over the edge. They never quite explained why they were in the act of 'arresting' him near the edge of a cliff."

Jerry stared at him, shocked at the directness of his words. Weakening in the knees a little, he sat in the chair.

Connors saw how he looked and went over to shelf for a pitcher of water. He poured some into a glass, walked over to Jerry, and handed it to him. Jerry glanced at him but shook his head. Connors then set the glass on his desk and put his hand on Jerry's shoulder.

He said gently, "I know what it's like to lose a father. Only mine fell off his horse during the spring roundup."

Jerry said softly, "But yours wasn't murdered, not like this."

"No. But I still felt his loss, I assure you."

"I don't doubt it." Then Jerry rose and faced him. "From what I've heard, McDermott pays five dollars a day to his killers, not including fifty dollars for every man he kills. What I want to know from you is, who claimed that money?"

Connors looked at him levelly and answered, "A man named Al Hardy. There's a rumor that two other men actually did it, but they disappeared and Hardy just ordered it."

"That doesn't make him any less guilty, does it?"

"No, it doesn't."

Jerry took his derby off his desk and went to the door.

Connors worriedly asked, "Where are you going?"

Jerry looked at him bitterly and asked, "What do you think?"

Connors saw the man's eyes and paused before he spoke.

"Now wait a minute, Bingham," he said urgently. "You don't know what you're doing. Hardy's always surrounded by his men, and if you think they're going to let you two fight fair and square, you're dead wrong! They'll pile on you and put a knife in your ribs before anyone can see who did it. Believe me, I know these people. You don't think I tried to get witnesses to testify against McDermott's crew? Behind their backs, the people of this town gripe about them, but to their faces, they bow and scrape and kowtow like some Negro servant before the war. I've just been on this job myself for two months and the only crimes they allow me to prosecute are rustling and horse-stealing, the prosecution of which benefits *them*, the cattlemen. Marshal Rawlins won't back me up, and if I step out of line, they might throw *me* over a cliff!   And that wouldn't do anyone a bit of good, least of all *me*!"

Jerry looked at him wryly, "Duly noted, counselor.   But I thought you wanted an ally to help you fight them."

"I do! But we're going to have to handle this a lot more quietly than you're planning on doing."

Jerry started out the door when Connors asked, "And what about filing on your father's land? Legally, it's yours now."

"Right now, I have more important business, Mister Connors." He put on his derby and left.

Connors watched him go and wondered if he should have told Jerry about Al Hardy. He was already painfully aware that far too many of the people he tried to enlist as allies ended up not coming back.

He had gone to three different saloons on three different streets, not to get a drink, but to ask the barmen if Al Hardy was there and if they could point him out. They all said that he hadn't been there but would give him a message. Jerry just thanked them and left, leaving no name or the reason why he wanted to see him.

Then, a half hour later, as he walked down Fairmont Street, wondering which saloon to hit next, he heard their horses approaching from down the street. He looked up and saw the riders practically roaring into town, hooting and hollering. Jerry surmised there must've been a dozen of them, and by their demeanor it was obvious that they thought they ran the town and that everyone else should just get out of their way. Jerry quickened his pace down the boardwalk to get closer to wherever they would stop.

He immediately saw the two men in the lead. One had black hair and a black moustache. "Looked like a vulture," was how the late Tom Tenney had described him. The other had "blond hair and a down-home accent, maybe Texas". Jerry had no idea exactly what a Texan sounded like, except maybe that he had a drawl; but there was no mistaking the blond-haired man riding next to the one who resembled a vulture.

The crew had stopped before the first saloon Jerry had gone to. As he watched these arrogant men, the rage was growing steadily within him and he noted the stiffness in his gait as he got closer to the two riders in the forefront of the group. He saw them dismount and went right up to the blond-haired man.

Al Hardy's feet had barely touched the ground when Jerry asked curtly, "Are you Al Hardy?"

Hardy still had the reins in his hand, and he was about to tie his mount to the hitching rail when Jerry accosted him. He stared at Jerry, trying to remember where he had seen him before. Quinn was standing just a few feet away and was also about to tie his horse to the rail, but his mind worked quicker than Hardy's, and he already recognized who Jerry was.

Before Quinn could speak, though, Hardy answered, "Yeah, that's me. Who the hell are you?"

Quinn asked, "Don't you see the family resemblance, Al?"

Hardy looked at Quinn oddly.

Jerry said tightly, "I'll give you a clue."

Then he punched Hardy in the face. The gunman fell back against his horse and the animal screamed at the impact.

Recovering quickly, Hardy whipped Jerry about the head and shoulders as the New Yorker shielded himself with his arms. Then, ducking low, Jerry grabbed Hardy around the midsection and both of them slammed into the gunman's horse. Screaming again, the animal moved back and, with nothing to lean against, the two men fell to the ground and rolled under the horse, punching and grappling.

Their hats had now fallen off and the two men on the ground

rolled over each other as the horse's hooves lifted and fell danger-ously close to them. Quinn and the other riders came forward and watched.

After a few seconds, Quinn said, "Enough of this rasslin' match. Get them outta there and snuff that dude out."

A few men started to move forward, but the frightened horse danced nervously towards them, forcing them to back away.

Then the two men on the ground suddenly rolled out into the street, kicking up clouds of dust into the air. A crowd started to form across the street and, despite the presence of Quinn and his men, they started to cheer loudly for Jerry.

With their arms still locked around each other the two men struggled to their feet, their fingers clawing each other's faces in an attempt to do as much damage as possible. Quinn watched them closely, looking for an opening when the two would separate and they could gun down Jerry without hitting Hardy. He could always claim later than he had seen Jerry reach for a knife.

The two men were now clear across the street and both tripped on the edge of the boardwalk and fell against a tie rail. Hardy's right hand was covering Jerry's face and pushing him as far back as he could, while at the same time, he tried to reach for his gun with his other hand.

Without seeing it, Jerry felt the other man going for his gun and he pushed Hardy over so that the gunman would be on his back against the tie rail. The pressure of the struggle was too much for the old rail and it collapsed noisily under them. Being on the bottom, Hardy's back hit the hard boardwalk and he cried out in pain. With Jerry's weight pressing down on him, Hardy had no room to draw.

Angrily, Jerry raised himself up and punched the gunman in the eye. Furiously, he kept punching Hardy again and again, the rage within him not abating until he drew blood.

Across the street, Quinn cocked the hammer of his .45 and took aim at Jerry's back.

Suddenly, he heard the roar of trace chains and horses' hooves coming closer. He shot a look to his right and saw the three o'clock stage from Omaha barreling down the street, its driver hollering at the top of his lungs. To further motivate his animals in getting to the stage station on time, the driver snapped a rattlesnake bullwhip just above their sweating backs.

Quinn pointed the gun skyward and stepped back just as horses and stagecoach rumbled past them.

After it passed completely, Quinn saw the two fighting men now on their feet, only Jerry was holding up Hardy as he kept punching him in the face. Quinn could see that the gunman's face was bloody and unrecognizable. Hardy lifted his arms feebly at Jerry, but he was quickly losing consciousness as the New Yorker continued to make short work of his face.

After he gave Hardy a punishing blow to the stomach, Jerry threw a hard-right cross to the man's already bloodied nose. Hardy fell back against the building wall and slid down to the ground. Jerry was breathing hard as he looked down at Hardy, his fists still clenched as he half-expected the gunman to rise suddenly for a sneak attack. Only when he saw that Hardy wasn't faking and that he was truly out for the duration did he relax.

Quinn said angrily, "Come on!"

He stepped further into the street and the other riders started to follow him until a rifle bullet hit the ground before them. Quinn's eyes darted around the street, but he couldn't see where the shot had come from.

Seeing that the shot didn't come from Quinn or his men, Jerry backed against the building's wall, bewildered as to who would have the nerve to fire at McDermott's crew. The crowd watching the fight scattered in all directions as even more shots were fired.

Quinn and the riders all had their guns out and whirled around helplessly, wondering where the shots were coming from. They were fired methodically, all of them aimed, not at Quinn or his men, but at the skittish horses behind them. With bullets splattering off the ground around them, the panicky horses, most of whom were standing free since Jerry had interrupted the crew in the act of tying them to hitching rails, broke from their owners and in a bunch fled down the street at a fast gallop.

Quinn cursed furiously as he saw the horses barreling their way out of town. He screamed, "Hell with Al! Get them damn horses!" They all holstered their guns and quickly ran up the street after their runaway mounts.

Many in the crowd, hiding indoors or behind walls, couldn't help laughing as they watched the crew head out of town on foot.

Meanwhile, in an alley between Timothy Jones' barber shop and Creighton's Funeral Parlor, Connors, now wearing his coat and Stetson, calmly reloaded his smoking rifle.

Then, he nonchalantly stepped out of the mouth of the alley and right in the path of a little blond-haired boy, about nine years old, munching on a stick of licorice. Connors stared at the boy, who looked up at him innocently.

Then, before Connors could speak, the boy drawled, "It's all right, mister. I didn't see nothing."

Connors stepped up to the boy, patted him on the head and said, "Good boy."

He turned and started to walk away until he remembered something.

"By the way," he added, "It's 'I didn't see *any*thing'."

Jerry saw the men running out of town, then scanned the buildings around him but couldn't see who his benefactor was.

The clop of stamping feet on the boardwalk made him turn around and he saw Jill running towards him.

"Jerry!" she cried as she threw herself in his arms and hugged him tightly.

"I was just coming from the Cattlemen's House when I saw the fight. I thought they were going to kill you!"

Jerry gently stroked her hair and said, "I have a feeling they would have, except for that guardian angel who fired those shots."

Jill said excitedly, "I heard 'em too. I don't know who it could have been, but you were crazy to start a fight with Al Hardy when his men were all around him."

She looked up at him then, and quickly saw the anger within him.

Jerry said earnestly, "Al Hardy was the one who had my dad thrown off a cliff. And if I miss my guess, he was the same man who killed Tommy and his parents. He certainly fits the description Tommy said. And that dark-haired vulture next to him must've been—"

"Charlie Quinn," she said.

He nodded, his eyes getting lost in hers.

"You must have heard the town gossip about Hardy killing your father."

"Not really. I got the information from Bill Connors."

Jill pulled out of his embrace and said angrily, "Connors! He the cattlemen's bought and paid-for city attorney! That man's been on their payroll since he got the job a couple months back. What the hell did you see him for?"

"I wanted to find out a few things, like who killed my father." He looked down at Hardy, still unconscious on the ground.

Jill looked at the gunman with contempt and said, "I never thought I'd see anyone get the best of him." Then she bent over, yanked his gun out of his holster and stood erect. She asked, "What're you going to do with him?"

"Put him in jail for murder."

She shook her head at his naiveté.

"Rawlins will never arrest him. Believe me, Jerry, even if he makes a show of putting him in a cell, after you leave, he'll give him a gun and let him go."

"Not if Connors backs me up."

Jill shook her head again and gave him a grave smile.

"That man does not want to die. He'll never do it."

"Let's find out. First, let's find something to tie his hands with."

Jerry was glad that Connors' office was just up the block; he hated to think of the trouble of dragging Hardy halfway across town.

The attorney stood up from his desk and gaped at them as they entered.

"What the hell is this?" he asked indignantly.

Hardy had his hands tied behind his back with his own necker-chief and they were holding him by his arms as they dragged him in. His face was covered with bruises and his eyes seemed to be half-shut; dried blood darkened his upper lip beneath his nose.

After yanking him in through the open door, Jerry shoved him onto a leather couch against the wall. The gunman looked up at him sullenly.

"You're a dead man, Bingham," he said. "You're gonna go over a cliff just like your old man."

Jerry started to move towards him, but before he could, Jill stepped in and slapped the gunman hard across the mouth. Hardy's eyes shut tight and he turned away as he withstood the slap.

Jill said bitterly, "I'm sorry I can't do to you what you did to Tommy, but that'll do for now."

Connors said, "Why did you bring him up here?"

Jerry paused to take a breath. His own face was scratched and bruised, and his coat was caked with dust and torn at the shoulder. He hadn't retrieved his hat which was still lying back on the street.

He said, "I want him put in jail."

Connors stared at him as if he was crazy. "Then bring him to Rawlins. I'm not the marshal."

Jill said, "You know Rawlins won't put him in a cell, Connors."

Sarcastically, Connors replied, "And what do you want me to do? Build my own jail?"

Jerry cut in. "You're the city prosecutor. Can't you order Rawlins to jail Hardy?"

"On what charge?"

"*Murder*, remember? You told me that Hardy killed my father."

"I told you a *rumor*! Charlie Quinn said it was an accident, and there are no witnesses that say otherwise. What I mentioned to you was just hearsay; there's absolutely no concrete proof that Al Hardy accepted payment for a killing. I can't indict a man on idle gossip!"

"*Idle gossip*! You're weaseling your way out of this, Connors. For God's sakes, didn't you just hear Hardy threaten me with the same kind of death my father got?"

Connors looked at Hardy glaring at him and tried not to swallow nervously in front of them.

He faced Jerry and said, "Apparently, you've assaulted him in some way and naturally he's mad at you. So—"

Jill finished it for him. "So, in other words, folks say things when they're riled that they don't really mean."

"*Exactly*!" said Connors. "What he just said is inadmissible in court."

"Jesus!" cried Jerry. "This is the only town in the country where everyone knows a murderer is walking among them and they accept it!"

"Again," said Connors, "*rumor*, Mister Bingham, not proven fact. And you can't grab someone off the street and tie them up just because of a baseless suspicion. It becomes an illegal incarceration, otherwise known as a kidnapping. The marshal would be in his rights to arrest you then."

Angrily, Jill said, "You see, Jerry? I said he was in their pocket! I knew bringing him up was a waste of time!"

Connors said with false indignation, "Miss Carmody, I'll pretend I didn't hear that. Now I strongly suggest you cut this man loose before *he* brings charges against *you*."

Jerry said through his teeth, "I'd rather die than release this murdering bastard."

"Then leave him here and I'll cut him loose."

Jill said, "Come on, Jerry!"

She turned and was about to leave when she spat thickly at Hardy's face. The gunman growled angrily, pulling at his ropes.

"You'll die for that!" he screamed. "Both of you! I'm gonna do you both and it won't be pretty!"

Jerry turned to Connors and said, "And that's not a threat?"

The attorney replied, "The woman *spat* on him! What do you expect him to say?"

With a frustrated roar, Jerry threw up his hands and turned to follow Jill out the door. Then his eyes went to the far side of the office and he suddenly spotted Connors' rifle leaning against the wall. A realization came to him then and he wanted to look back at Connors, but he was well aware that Hardy was still glaring at him. So, he just left without a glance in the attorney's direction.

After he left, Hardy rose and turned his tied hands towards Connors as the attorney came around the desk with a letter opener.

"Thanks, Connors," he said. "At least, *you* know which side of the street to play on."

As he cut the neckerchief apart, Connors said, "I've always been loyal to the Combine, Hardy, you know that..."

Free of his bonds, Hardy felt his wrists and looked at Connors. The attorney couldn't miss the rage in the man's eyes.

"I've got a score to settle with that dude and that homesteader bitch. And, frankly, I don't care *what* you make out of that statement with your lawyer double-talk."

Then he went out the door before Connors could reply.

After a moment, Connors shut the door, walked over to his rifle and picked it up. He put his fingers on the iron barrel and felt that it was still hot.

Quietly, he said, "The law is a two-edged sword, my friend..."

CHAPTER SIX

"THIS IS GETTING OUT OF CONTROL!"

That was Peter Ridgeway, the one who stuck his foot out and tripped Jill at the Cattlemen's House.

They were all seated in various plush chairs around McDermott's living room. Predictably, Tad McDermott was seated in the biggest chair in the room, the one in front of the fireplace and beneath the picture of the old Scottish warrior swinging his huge sword.

McDermott blew out a large cloud of cigar smoke. His eyes were slits through the billowing clouds. "Once again, gentlemen," he said sarcastically, "Mister Ridgeway has blessed us with his uncanny insight into our affairs." Ridgeway's face reddened.

McDermott said, "Gentlemen, we've got something much worse than cow fever to deal with. We're facin' another kind of disease. And that disease is called *defiance*."

Seated at the other end of the room, Len Cagle noted the men around the room becoming alert, the slight shifting forward in their cushy chairs.

McDermott's eyes went to Eugene Farnsworth, who was pouring himself a brandy.

"Gene," he said, trying to restrain the fury in his voice, "before, your daughter was just a big pain in the butt sidin' with the homesteaders and complainin' about all the big, bad things the cattlemen are doin' to the valley. But Bingham's son has lit a fire under her. In fact, the two of them together have been the biggest thorns in the side of the Combine since that blizzard the winter before last killed off thousands of cattle and almost put us out of business."

Honus Wilder asked, "But why, Tad? Because Bingham's son beat up Reed and then Al Hardy—"

Cagle interrupted him, his voice sounding sharp and condescending to the others in the room.

"Al Hardy is not an easy man to defeat, Mister Wilder, especially in physical combat. I first knew him as a towheaded boy who rode for Bloody Bill Anderson. He did more than his share of killing in Lawrence in Sixty-three. When the blue-bellies were chasing us, he stayed in the saddle for seven and a half hours straight until we got back to Lone Jack, Missouri. I saw him personally decapitate Union soldiers at Centralia and play a macabre game of putting one soldier's head on another's headless body." He leaned back in his chair with a slight smile. He was obviously enjoying the fact that his grotesque story was making the cattlemen uncomfortably shift in their chairs. McDermott, however, just puffed on his cigar, undisturbed by his aide's story. In fact, he thoroughly enjoyed seeing his men go at each other like rabid dogs fighting over a bone. To him, anger was good, and for his men to duke it out, whether verbally or physically, made them all the more stronger.

After an awkward pause, Judge Alcott said, "All this may be true, Mister Cagle. However, all this says about Al Hardy is that he enjoys tormenting and murdering men he has unfair advantage of, whether by force of arms or by the numbers of men on his side. That's not a warrior, Mister Cagle, that's a bully."

Cagle glared at him and his Adam's apple bobbed in his throat as if it wanted release.

Yet Judge Alcott ignored this and continued.

"If what you say about Hardy is true, then one should be doubly impressed by Jerry Bingham. He beat Mister Hardy in a fair fight without either guns or numbers on his side."

"That ain't true," said McDermott. "There was one man, Lord knows who he is, who fired a rifle at my crew and kept them from helpin' Al. It was the first time anyone, and I mean *anyone*, in this poor excuse for a town had lifted a finger against my boys.   And that, gentlemen, is the crux of the matter.   This Bingham and Gene's daughter have planted the seed of defiance in this town. Someone, we don't know who it is, has decided to buy in when Hardy was gettin' a lickin'.   And that we cannot allow! Tell 'em why, Len."

Cagle, still smarting from Judge Alcott's rebuttal to his praise of Al Hardy, gladly complied.

"Because," he said crisply, "if we, that is, the Combine, accept even one townsman thwarting our plans, then others will think we're weak and follow suit. Any fear we have fostered by our rule will be gone and, when the people once again find their spines, they will attack us and wipe us out. I've even heard a rumor that sheepherders were taking over ranges up north and moving further and further south every spring. You know what that means. Our grass and water will be gone and with it, our business-es. If we don't provoke fear, unrestrained naked *fear* on our enemies, no matter who they are, townsmen, homesteaders, sheepherders, then we may as well pack up and leave this land and never return."

To the men around the room, it was a chilling pronouncement.

"So," added McDermott, "this is about more than just the one hundred sixty or so acres of land Bingham's son will inherit from his father. We've got to cut the snake's head off! Now!"

Farnsworth asked timidly, "Does Jill come into that category too?" All eyes looked to him when he asked the question; then, as if on cue, they all swiveled their heads back to Tad McDermott for his answer.

After casually flicking a cigar ash into an ashtray, he looked at the burning end and said, "There must be sacrifices in any war, Gene." Then his eyes locked on him from across the room. "I heard you say, many, many, *many* times—'I have no daughter!' Now, I don't give a damn whether you're sayin' that to us or whether you're tryin' to convince yourself, one thing is damn certain: There's not goin' to be a debate about it. She dies. I don't care how, and I don't care where, but I want her in the ground, and that goes double for George Bingham's kid. Take those two out of the runnin' permanently and the people of this town will go back to bein' brainless sheep." He looked around the room. "Agreed, gentlemen?"

After an uncomfortable pause, the other cattlemen nodded and voiced their assent; that is, all except Eugene Farnsworth.

McDermott stared at him. "Gene? I didn't hear a 'yes'."

They all looked at Farnsworth.

He hesitated for just a moment before he slowly nodded his head.

"Yes, Tad. We'll do it *your* way."

With the butt of the cigar still between his teeth, McDermott grinned and said, "Of course."

Cagle leaned forward in his chair and said, "But the important thing now is to concoct some justification for their murders. Both of them are getting some admiration around town. Folks may not like hearing about their sudden deaths. It might even empower the homesteaders further."

McDermott asked, "Then what's your plan, Len?"

Cagle's eyes shone and his enthusiasm grew as he spoke.

"Well, we've already been painting the homesteaders as the rustling element. Jill Carmody herself has complained about it far too many times already. However, now we're going to go even further. Make Jill Carmody and Jerry Bingham the heads of a gang of rustlers. It'll be a huge gang, all-powerful, with friends in high places. They steal us blind; hundreds of head go missing, and besides that, the gang has threatened to assassinate all the heads of the cattle outfits."

McDermott nodded and said, "Sounds good. But will the suckers in town fall for it?"

Cagle answered, "We control the press in Starrett City, and we have the sympathies of other newspapers around the state. Say something enough times, and a body will believe it because he has nothing else to fall back on."

McDermott grinned and said, "These rabble in town are pretty easy to convince. They're like dogs chasin' their tails 'cause they can't see what's around them."

"What we have to continue to do," added Cagle, "is see that they never stop chasing their tails."

It was the perfect moment for a knock on the door. Bennett, McDermott's butler, answered it.

The men soon heard a Swedish-accented voice say, "Thank you."

Kinderstrom entered the room, hatless and out of breath. He dropped into an empty chair. When Bennett offered him a tray with brandy, he shook his head and the butler left the room.

McDermott looked at him irritably. "Nice of you to join us, Ches. Hope we're not keepin' you from any important business."

Kinderstrom looked at him pointedly, not missing the sarcasm in his tone. The Swede's face was bruised from his fight with Jerry and his falling through the window of the newspaper office. His right hand had a thick white bandage tied around it.

McDermott said testily, "You were also supposed to travel up to Omaha and grease some palms. If we're goin' to make hay on defeatin' this damn Homesteaders' Act, we need more folks in the legislature on our side. But you said you couldn't do the trip and instead you wanted to meet with us. Okay, we're all here, bright-eyed and bushy-tailed, now what the hell is on your mind?"

He saw McDermott's rage and hesitated but decided to plow through anyway.

"I'm quitting," he said.

The men around the room made quiet remarks to each other. Len Cagle and his boss just stared at Kinderstrom as if he were some kind of leper.

Finally, McDermott shouted, "Shut up! All of you! This ain't a damn beauty parlor with a buncha chatterin' females!"

Then he fixed Kinderstrom with a level stare and asked, "And if I may inquire, especially after puttin' us through the expense of bringin' you clear across the ocean and installin' you as the head of the Sentinel, just *why* you're doin' this?"

No one could miss the venom beneath the sarcasm. The nervous cattlemen practically held their collective breaths waiting for the Swede to answer.

After a sizable pause, Kinderstrom finally replied, "There are several reasons. One is physical illness. I seriously hurt my back in that fight with Bingham. That crash through the window of the newspaper office has scarred me, I think, in mind as well as body. I've seen Doctor Griffin and he's done his best, but, let's face it, he's prairie trash and not a big-city doctor. He can't stop this persistent pain in my lower back. He can't cure this...this fear I now have of getting involved in any more physical skirmishes with these wild, undisciplined people in this country. I've never gotten into any physical confrontations with farmers in Europe, much less crashed through a storefront window. I've never faced such rage before, no matter how embittered the enemy was. But these...American ruffians!"

McDermott leaned forward, his cigar still balanced between his fingers. His expression was tight, and his eyes bore into the Swede intently.

He said, "Let me tell you somethin', Kinderstrom. When I came out here with Maria many years ago, we faced the Arapahos and the Cheyenne. Now I heard that the Apaches are bigger sons of bitches, but you couldn't convince me of it, not when the Cheyenne gutted my men like fish. So, what was I supposed to do, let the red niggers chase us back east with our tails between our legs? That was *not* an option, Mister Kinderstrom. I went out and hired men who had iron in them, *real iron*! Like *me*! We rode out, the bunch of us, to the Cheyenne camps. We cut their women up like slabs of beef and smashed their children's skulls against the trunks of trees. So, what of it? They did that to us, and we paid them in kind. And their so-called warriors? We saw their insides! We cut off pieces of their bodies *slowly* so they could stop and think about what they're goin' through. Their bones are now somewhere out there bleachin' in the sun. You must steel your heart to be in our business, Kinderstrom. I don't need any *women* on my payroll!"

Kinderstrom scowled at him, not missing the insult.

The cattlemen around the room, however, were sickened by McDermott's story, and all of them tried to ignore what the story implied about their leader's psyche. Cagle, however, was smiling at their discomfort.

Kinderstrom rose and said icily, "Your story just demonstrated to me the level of class you've always had, Mister McDermott."

McDermott glared at the Swede as he arrogantly stood facing him from across the room.

Kinderstrom added, "And furthermore, I've been gauging public opinion, both in this town and among the local govern-ments around the state. You are *not* admired, sir; neither is your Combine. Many of these people want you to go and go quickly. In fact, I suspect that officials in Omaha will not be on your side no matter what you pay them. And if I cannot influence them, what further purpose is there for me to stay?"

"And what will you do?" asked Wilder. "Return to Stockholm?"

Kinderstrom responded, "I'll go to some big city in the east and get in good with the political establishment there. Anything's better than living with these saddle trash....Nevertheless, I'm still entitled to some money for the services I've rendered to you and your Combine..."

Putting down his cigar, McDermott rose to his feet. Then he picked up his half-full glass of brandy and raised it.

"Gentlemen!" he said.

Everyone in the room likewise rose to his feet and obediently lifted their glasses.

McDermott said, "To Ches Kinderstrom!"

He drained his glass. The others toasted the Swede as well and finished their brandies.

Then, after McDermott put down his glass, he drew a .45 Colt from his shoulder holster and shot Kinderstrom in the chest.

The others stared at the scene in horror. Kinderstrom stood there for just a second or two, a look of shock across his thin face as he grasped his bloody chest. Then he dropped to the carpeted floor with a thud.

McDermott shouted, "Bennett!"

The butler entered the room.

"Clean that up."

Without pause, Bennett proceeded to lift Kinderstrom's dead body off the floor and drag him away, albeit awkwardly. All eyes followed him as he left the room.

McDermott said cheerily, "And there, gentlemen, is our ace in the hole."

Ridgeway said, "Kinderstrom's dead body? I don't see how—"

"I think I see what Tad is getting at," Cagle said. "To portray Jill Farnsworth and Jerry Bingham as rustlers is one thing..."

McDermott finished the sentence for him.

"But now," he added smugly, "we have given our public a *corpse!*"

CHAPTER SEVEN

THEY WERE RIDING BACK ON THE OPEN PLAIN WITH THE SUN AT their backs. It was on the lee side of the afternoon and the warmest part of the day. Jill had removed her vest and folded it under her saddle and her Stetson was off. Sweat stained her ranch shirt and she felt aches all over her body from the encounter with McDermott at the Cattlemen's House, especially her stomach.

Jerry's face was still bruised from the fight. At least he was able to go back to the hotel and retrieve his belongings which were now in a carpetbag tied to his saddle, and pay his bill. He had been able to retrieve his derby and also change into a new coat since the old one was ripped up from the fight. Wryly, he reflected that being a man in the west and fighting for your principles took a heavy toll, not on one's spirit, but on one's clothes.

"You know, Jill," he said, "you don't have to do this. I still think I would have been safe at the hotel."

"Believe me, Jerry," she replied, "if I know those bastards, putting a chair against the door of your room would *not* have stopped McDermott's boys from getting in there and murdering you. And as long as I'm around, I'm not going to let that happen."

Jerry stared at her, trying to see what was in her eyes; but she suddenly realized what she had blurted out and purposely avoided eye contact, finding a reason to stare at a lone mountain a dozen miles away.

They were silent for a few minutes. Then Jerry asked, "What happened up in the Cattlemen's House?"

Jill didn't look at him when she answered. "I just told them off."

"That's all?"

"That's all."

Jerry stared at her, again trying to gauge something from her face.

Suddenly he said, "Baloney!"

Jill looked at him oddly.

Seeing her look, he said, "It's what they call a 'cold cut'. It's a kind of meat they serve back east in certain restaurants."

She said wryly, "Folks must look down upon it then since it means a lie."

Jerry said gently, "Jill, I wish you'd trust me."

Jill didn't respond. Deep down, she was still wondering if she should tell him what happened. She wanted to be honest with Jerry, but she had just seen how he acted when he found out that Al Hardy had murdered his father. He may have been a man from the east, a corporate attorney who had worked on high-class Fifth Avenue in Manhattan, but his reaction was that of a westerner who worked the cow trails all his life. Before he brought Hardy up to Connors' office, Jerry didn't call for a policeman or take his accusations to the proper authorities (which in reality, were nonexistent in that town). His first impulse was to go out and challenge the guilty party to a fistfight like any other man who worked all his life from dawn to dusk for little pay and an unpromising future. She smiled to herself as she thought about it; Jerry Bingham was more of a western man than even he realized.

However, the last thing Jill wanted was for him to once again take matters into his own hands and fight for her honor—not if he got himself killed in the process, that is.

She sighed.

"Leave it alone, Jerry," she said wearily. "Let's just get back to the cabin..."

They were camped a few miles west of Pawnee Creek, dirty, ornery and bone tired.

They had murdered another settler and his family and were riding back into town, but instead of a much-deserved meal and several bottles of good whiskey, they were accosted by some fancy-Dan from the east and forced to chase their runaway horses all over the valley to get them back.

If that wasn't enough, their boss sends out a rider to tell them *not* to return to the ranch, but instead to ride out to the Carmodys' place and take care of even more business. For Charlie Quinn, it was enough to almost make him chuck it all and tell Tad McDermott to do his own killing.

But in his heart, he knew he couldn't do that since he had discovered, to his surprise, that he liked the act of killing more than he cared to admit.

He sat on the edge of the cook fire, a tin mug of coffee in his hand as he watched the dying embers and heard them audibly crackle and hiss. The others were scattered around, some using their saddles for pillows and catching a much-needed snooze, and others standing around fortifying themselves with quick bites of beef jerky and cups of steaming black coffee with shots of whiskey furtively poured in so Charlie wouldn't notice.

Quinn thought of all the killing he had done and all the killing he had watched and approved of and, in rare, quiet moments, his mind drifted back to that day twenty-six years ago when he was eight and the world looked like one big playroom to romp around in. The game was so innocent at first, and so simple that it almost frightened him how easy it was to play it. *Go ahead*, sneered his big brother, *I'll let you have first draw*. It was only a game, he told himself. *Jeez, everyone in town carried guns; they shot at each other in saloons, on the streets, and in each other's homes; hell, it was a part of all their lives*. Hank was a boastful, arrogant son of a bitch and he never liked him. He bullied him mercilessly, made his mom's life hell and tried desperately to imitate their late father, a no-good drunken brawler who met his match in a saloon gunfight.

They both had guns in their waistbands and both boys were ready to draw on each other, except for one difference: Hank's gun was a realistic-looking toy and Charlie's was the real one his father had hidden in the closet long before he died. After Hank called it, they whipped out their respective pistols and while Hank said, "Bang!" a bullet hit him square in the right eye and came out the back of his skull. Their mother ran in and gaped at the sight. She screamed at him and called him every name in the book and then some. Then she came out with a word that shook him up and never left him from that day on. Insane. Young as he was, he knew what it meant; not right in the head, touched, in need of help. One who was "insane" had to be taken away from others and put in the bughouse for the rest of his days. It unnerved him just to think about it. After she said the horrible word, his mother swung her hand back and then slammed him hard in the face. The blow sent him across the room where he crashed into some wooden chairs. His head was pounding, and he sat up on the floor, blood all over his mouth.

Then, as she rushed towards him, she said it again. Insane.

So, he raised the gun and shot her in the mouth.

After she fell back onto the kitchen floor, he rose from the ground and walked over. Looking down at her, he saw the blood and gore where her face used to be, but he never forgot the vacant stare of her still-open eyes as they gazed up at the ceiling.

Charlie Quinn glanced back at the saddle on the ground behind him and thought of the flask hidden there. He wondered if he should spike his coffee with a shot of whiskey but decided not to. He was a stickler for his men not drinking while they were on a raid, and he didn't want anyone to see him do it, so, reluctantly, he sipped his coffee plain.

Not far away from him, Al Hardy was sitting up on the ground smoking a cigarette. His eyes were little slits staring at nothing. Quinn noted his far-away look and knew full well what he was thinking. Al Hardy, number two ramrod in McDermott's elite crew of efficient killers, had been shown up, and shown up good. He was beaten in a fair fight by some dude from the east who didn't use a gun. Quinn knew what that was like. The others in the crew said nothing, but Quinn caught their little side glances and derisive sneers when Hardy passed them. The man had lost face with his crew, and when that happened, the next thing was orneriness, defiance of his orders and then outright rebellion among the whole lot of them.

It was never good for a bully to lose face with his men. To one who lived the dangerous life of killing for killing's sake, it was the beginning of the end.

Phil Devery was passing by and, tired and not really watching where he walked, accidentally kicked the toe of Hardy's boot as he stepped over his legs. It was a minor mishap, and would have been ignored in a moment, but not this time.

"Hey!" shouted Hardy.

Devery had already passed him and it took a moment before he realized that Hardy was addressing him. He turned around and sullenly asked, "Yeah?"

"Why don't you watch where you're goin'? You blind or somethin'!"

Devery just grinned at him. Then he looked at the others who stopped what they were doing and watched them. They were also starting to grin derisively.

Facing Hardy, he said, "What're you goin' to do about it, big man? Beat me with your little fists like you took care o' that dude?"

The others in the crew didn't blatantly laugh out loud, but some of them did snigger and the rest of them just grinned. At that point, they were willing to make fun of Hardy; but most of them were still afraid of Charlie Quinn, a man whom they knew was mad as a hatter.

Hardy got to his feet so fast that Devery barely had time to react when the gunman's fist hit him square on the nose. Not pausing for a moment, Hardy then grabbed a fistful of Devery's calico shirt with one hand and then drew his gun with the other.

The others in the crew stared at them now, no longer grinning.

Quinn merely drained the rest of his coffee and idly watched.

Hardy brought the heavy iron barrel down on the other man's forehead with a sickening thud. Devery's hat flew off and blood appeared on his scalp as he started to sag to the ground. But Hardy wasn't through.

He threw the unconscious man to the ground and then went down on his knees. Leaning over him, he raised the gun and brought it down again and again on Devery's head, the gun barrel fully soaked with blood.

On the eighth stroke, Quinn said quietly, "Okay, Al, that's enough. He's deader'n Lincoln. You can stop now..."

But Hardy didn't stop. Sweat was rolling off his face and his breathing was fast; he grunted loudly as he kept striking what was left of the dead man's skull.

Quinn looked at the others and said evenly, "All of you get some sleep before we ride out. I need y'all rested for what we've got to do..." Then, as if to provide an example, he threw his coffee grinds into the fire and lay back on the ground as if to prepare for sleep. As he did so, he privately hoped the nightmares wouldn't come this time.

Seeing this, the others in the group gradually stopped watching Hardy and quietly walked back to their respective plots of ground to lie down and get some sleep as well. By the time Hardy stopped pistol-whipping the dead man, some of the crew were already fast asleep. Others, however, just lay back with their eyes wide open staring up at the late afternoon sky; they would have trouble shutting them for a while...

They had taken the long way to get back to the cabin. They couldn't help it; it was a beautiful day and the ride through the valley took their minds off their troubles, if only temporarily. It was already late afternoon when they finally arrived. After they tied up their horses, Jill was about to enter the cabin when she noticed something was wrong.

When he saw her hesitate, Jerry asked, "What's the matter?"

Jill's eyes scanned the area, and her gaze ultimately settled on the corral.

She asked excitedly, "Where are the damn horses?"

She ran over to the corral fence and pushed open the gate. Then she rushed into the barn, leaving the door wide open.

Jerry watched her and wondered what was going on. Then he heard her scream, though it sounded more in frustration than in fear. He ran over to the corral and into the barn.

The two of them stood there and looked into the semi-darkness, the odor of sod and horse manure heavy around them. They were shocked to see that every stall gate was wide open and not one horse was in any of them.

Agitated, Jill ran a hand back through her hair as her eyes scanned every stall.

"We've been robbed!"

Jerry cursed as he stared at the empty stalls.

Then Jill said excitedly, "Morg!"

She ran out of the barn and Jerry followed her. In seconds, she burst into the house and looked around. When she turned back to the kitchen table, she spotted the note. Grabbing it off the table, she read it quickly.

Jerry asked, "What is it? Is he all right?"

She angrily crumpled the note and said, "The bastard!"

"What?"

"He's in town! Drinking up a storm at some saloon, no doubt. Why couldn't he stay here and protect the place?"

"Jill, calm down."

"Calm down, my butt. Okay, the man's wife is dead, I'm sorry for it. But that's no excuse to chuck your responsibilities to our home! If he was here, this wouldn't have happened."

"Jill, I wish you'd give him the benefit of the doubt. The man's not supposed to be confined here the rest of his days."

Jill's eyes narrowed and she said irritably, "That kind of thinking *won't* get our horses back!"

She stomped over to the open doorway and went outside. Shaking his head, Jerry followed her. Then both of them were brought up short by the riders surrounding the place with guns pointed at them. In the forefront was Charlie Quinn. Hardy had already dismounted and was standing inside the front gate.

"Well, well," said Quinn, leaning forward in the pommel. "Look who's here. Our favorite pains in the ass."

Jill said angrily, "You took our horses."

Quinn replied, "We sent a man back to McDermott's place with the string. Don't worry, Tad will take care of him as if they were his own—which actually, they are right now."

Hardy moved forward then. Catching Jerry off-guard, he punched him in the face, knocking him heavily to the ground. As the New Yorker tried to pick himself up, Hardy came forward and swung back his boot to kick him in the face.

Before he could, though, Jill struck Hardy right in his already busted nose. The gunman screamed and staggered back, his hands quickly covering his face.

"Damn bitch!" he screamed.

Four other riders jumped down off their mounts and ran over. They grabbed Jerry and Jill and pulled the struggling pair out through the fence. As if on cue, the riders moved their horses back and revealed a buggy standing in the middle of the road. The rig was coal black and had two beautiful stallions tied before it.

Jerry stared at it and asked, "What's that for?"

Quinn casually rolled a cigarette and said, "Today, we're bein' real generous. We're goin' to take you two lovebirds on a romantic carriage ride."

Desperately, Jill asked, "What'd you do to Morgan?"

Hardy had his neckerchief held up to his bleeding nose.

He said thickly, "We'll catch up to him."

Quinn said curtly, "Al!" Then he faced Jill and said, "You worry about yourself, lady..."

Jill almost smiled; they didn't get her brother then.

Quinn lit his cigarette and then blew some smoke out into the late afternoon breeze.

"Boys," he said quietly, "put 'em in the buggy."

It was still bright and sunny out, but daylight didn't have long to go; the western sky was starting to light up in an orange glow. However, they were not able to enjoy this beautiful sight as they sat still in the buggy's seats, their hands tied behind their backs and guns trained on them as their conveyance moved further along the trail. A rider in front of the buggy had tied the horses' reins to his own saddle, forcing the rig to stay directly behind him.

They worriedly looked at each other.

Jill asked, "Where do you think they're taking us?"

Jerry had thoughts about that, and they weren't cheerful ones. So, he lied.

"Probably taking us to McDermott to figure out what to do with us."

Jill smiled gravely and shook her head.

"Nice try, Mister Bingham..."

He looked at her sadly and said, "Guess that wasn't very convincing, was it?"

"No, it wasn't." Then she smiled at him and added, "But thanks for trying anyway."

The group had traveled for over an hour; two horses tied to a buggy with two young people in it, and being pulled by one lone rider, and eight other men riding all around them with rifles across their laps waiting for them to make an attempt to get away.

Quinn and Hardy were riding in front of the group, their eyes scouting the surrounding hills for any signs of life.

Hardy was moody and irritable and had been that way since Jill had punched him in the nose; but something else was bothering him as well.

He said sullenly, "I don't know why I have to ride up here with you. Why can't I be back there with them?"

Quinn's eyes scanned the ridges and bluffs high above them as they passed through a narrow canyon.

"Because," he replied, "that rider Tad sent out to find us gave *me* the note and *I* read it, not you."

"Meanin'?"

"Meanin' you don't know what Tad wants us to do and *I* do."

"And that is?"

"Tad doesn't want them marked up in any way. That's why I stopped you from pistol-whippin' the daylights out of both of them back there..." He then looked at him deliberately. "...Like your late friend, Phil Devery."

Hardy looked down at his pommel for a moment.

Quietly, he said, "He was askin' for it."

"Yeah, well, now he's got it. Had to bury his sorry butt six feet under the dirt back there so no one'll find him. *That's* the main reason why you're up here with me sightseein'. You're on the prod, Al. I can't trust you to be a good boy around those two when Tad doesn't want them touched. Savvy?"

"But why? Doesn't he want those two in the ground?"

"'Course he does. But that note told me just how it's goin' to be done, and that means no other way but that."

"Then where are we takin' 'em?"

"Got to find the right spot. Somewhere far away from any folks who might be around. One thing is for sure, though."

"What's that?"

"They won't be comin' back..."

CHAPTER EIGHT

TWO HOURS EARLIER, CONNORS WAS LEAVING THE COURTHOUSE for the day when he ran into Judge Alcott at the front entrance.

He nodded and said, "Afternoon, Judge."

"Afternoon, Bill."

"You're showing up kind of late in the day."

"I know," the Judge said, out of breath. "Tad's got me working on a new article for the Sentinel. I was going to work on it up in my chambers."

"You? What happened to that Swedish character?" He snapped his fingers trying to remember the name. "Uh, Kindersun."

"Kinder*strom*," the judge corrected.

"Right, right, Kinderstrom. Why isn't he writing this...article?"

Judge Alcott paused for a moment and he avoided Connors' gaze.

"He's...gone upstate to see some legislators."

Connors watched him closely and almost felt like shaking his head at the judge's flustering manner. He was all-too familiar with

Alcott's lies, but they were usually meant for the public.   If Connors' guess was right, however, the old fool was lying now. Curiously, he started to wonder why.

"Oh?   And what's this item going to be about, as if I didn't know."

The judge sighed and said lamely, "Oh, you know, more stuff about the rustler element."

"Ahh," said Connors, as if he understood perfectly. He knew exactly how to work the judge. Well aware that Alcott could be a boastful old fool, Connors knew that by acting indifferently to what he was talking about, the old man would respond by jabbering away with no end in sight.

Seeing what he thought was a lack of interest on Connors' part, the Judge added, "Well, we've got to keep up the pressure on these rustlers. Especially those two young folks making so much trouble."

Connors paused before speaking, as if he didn't know who the old man was talking about.

"...Two young folks, you say?"

Judge Alcott grinned derisively and said, "Come on, Bill, you know who I'm talking about. Bingham's son and the Carmody girl."

Connors nodded as if a light had just gone on in his head.

"Of course! Those two!"

"I mean, you *should* be aware of the trouble they're causing. Al Hardy told us they were up in your office the other day trying to get you to put him in jail."

Connors said, "I'm sorry, Judge! It slipped my mind."

"Slipped your mind! Huh!"

"Anyway, I took care of it. They won't visit me again."

"I'll daresay they won't visit *anyone* again!"

Connors stared at him and asked, "Why is that, Judge?"

Judge Alcott paused, wondering if he had said too much; but his natural penchant for gab was overwhelming him.

Finally, the old man blurted out, "Because they're going to be hanged for Kinderstrom's murder!"

Connors was shaken by what the judge said and resisted the temptation to show his natural shock at the statement.

Instead, the attorney put on his poker face and said, "Kinder-sun's supposed to be—"

"Kinder*strom*!"

"Kinderstrom…is dead, yet he's supposed to be traveling upstate to meet with legislators. That's some trick."

"Well, all right," the judge said apologetically. "Guess I should've laid my cards on the table from the beginning."

"It never hurts."

The judge glanced around to make sure no one passing by in the street was listening.

"You see," he began in a confidential manner, "Bingham and the Carmody girl had a fight with Kinderstrom at the Sentinel office. So, it goes to figure that—"

Connors finished it. "That they murdered him."

"*Now* you've got it!"

"Of course," the attorney said wryly, "what flawless logic."

"We think so."

Connors idly looked around at the street before he asked the next question; as if he really didn't care one way or the other.

"And…you've scheduled a date for the trial?"

"What trial?"

Connors couldn't help staring at him this time.

He said, "The trial for Bingham and Carmody where they'll be accused of Kinderstrom's murder. I mean, I assume no matter what happens, you'll sentence them to hang, right?"

"The sentence should be carried out in another hour or so."

Connors stared at the man as if he were a leper. In all his life, he had never wanted to hit someone so much; but he had to hold his temper if he wanted more information from the old crook.

Again, his manner assumed a lack of interest.

"You're...sure of this?"

"Sure? I've just come for seeing Tad and the others now. He said that he sent Quinn, Hardy and some others in the crew out to pick them up at the girl's place. Then they're to take them way out in the hills and hang them both."

Connors took all this in and tried to not to show his concern. He knew that to do so would mean that it would get back to McDermott and his life wouldn't be worth a Confederate gold-piece.

"And they were sent out when?"

"Oh, I don't know; half hour ago, I guess."

"Well," said Connors evenly, "I see your work is cut out for you with that article."

"I'll say! I'm still trying to figure out where Quinn's crew found Kinderstrom's body."

"Why don't you say you found him in Pawnee Creek, with water flowing all over him?"

The judge pointed his finger at him and grinned. "Now that's a good idea! Lend a little melodrama to it."

"Could always use a little melodrama," Connors said gravely.

"I'll use that," said the judge, moving to leave.

"Good! Anyway, I'm kinda hungry."

"Sure, Bill. Go fill your belly. And thanks."

Connors smiled and said, "Anytime, Judge."

"See you later."

"Bye."

After Judge Alcott entered the courthouse, Connors dropped his smile and then turned back towards the street. He had remembered seeing a certain horse tied up outside the Quarter Moon. He thanked God the place was only a block away. Inwardly, he prayed that the horse and its owner would still be there.

He entered the Quarter Moon and shouldered his way through the mass of cowboys and gamblers, storekeepers and freighters, saloon girls and trollops, all bustling about in the large, smoke-filled room. It didn't take him long to find who he was looking for.

Connors maneuvered through the hardened bunch carefully; he didn't need to get into a mindless, time-wasting fistfight now, not when time was so precious.

Carefully, he made his way to the bar and stopped just a few inches behind Morgan Carmody. The young man was leaning on the bar, a glass of whiskey in his hand. He seemed to be lost in thought as he stared blankly at his reflection in the mirror.

Connors saw the empty look on his face and was praying that he wasn't totally into his cups. To his surprise, however, he saw that Morgan was alert enough to spot the attorney in the mirror.

Still facing the reflection, Morgan said idly, "I recognize you. You're Starrett City's renowned chief attorney. What's an impor-tant man like you doing in this den of inequity?"

Then he downed the whiskey in one quick gulp and reached for the bottle at his elbow.

Quickly, Connors put his hand on his arm.

The tone in Morgan's voice got nasty then. Swinging around to face the attorney, he said tautly, "You don't want to do that, friend."

Connors said earnestly, "It's best to keep you sharp for what you've got to do. That is, if you value your sister's life."

Morgan's anger faded all at once. "What did you say?"

Connors repeated, "Your sister's life, Carmody. They're going to kill her and Jerry Bingham if you don't put down that goddamn drink and help them."

Morgan seemed to be trying to focus his eyes on the attorney, as if he was waking up from a deep sleep.

"What're you talking about?"

Connors glanced about, seeing the crowd around them. Satisfied that his voice wouldn't carry over the din, he faced Morgan again and directed his words quietly, but firmly, to the man before him.

"McDermott's boys have gone to your place to grab Jill and Bingham, and from there they're going to take them somewhere to hang them. Now is that clear enough for you?"

Morgan's eyes widened in fear. Then he asked, "How do you know?"

"Never mind how I know," he said tensely. "The important question is, are you going to sit here and let them do it?"

For a moment, Morgan stared at the dirty wooden floor, as if he needed some time to absorb this new information.

Then, taking a different tack, Connors said gently, "I've heard about what you went through, Morgan. You don't want what happened to Emma Lou to happen to *Jill*, do you?"

Morgan looked up at him, his eyes sad at the mention of his dead wife.

"From our place, you say?"

Connors nodded and said, "You've still got an hour of daylight left."

Then Morgan felt his lack of confidence returning. When he spoke, it was as if Connors wasn't there.

"But how can I find them in all that wilderness?"

Connors said reassuringly, "You were a scout for the army. You tracked the Cheyenne through half the state day and night. It shouldn't take much for you to track a dozen or so horses while it's still light."

Morgan looked at the attorney again, and the two men stared at each other for a few seconds. Deep down, Connors was hoping that the old cavalry man that Morgan was would come to the fore.

Abruptly, Morgan reached into his pocket and tossed a coin on the bar as he rose from his seat.

He asked, "Are you coming with me?"

"I can't."

"Why not?"

"Because I've got to look like I have nothing to do with this."

"How do I know that you and McDermott are not luring me into some kind of trap?"

"You don't," Connors replied bluntly. "But I figure you'd never forgive yourself if I warned you about them being lynched and you did nothing to prevent it."

Morgan thought about that, but not for long.

Facing him, he answered, "Right again, Counselor..."

"All right," Quinn announced. "Right here will do."

After an hour and ten minutes of traveling all over the valley, the group had finally stopped at the edge of a grove of cottonwoods near the bottom of a lonely hill. In fact, the trees were so close to it that an outcropping of boulders sat beneath one particular tree its thick branches reaching out towards the hill itself.

The riders dismounted and tied their horses deeper back in the cottonwoods so they wouldn't be spotted. The men guarding the two young people leveled their rifles at them and one man ordered, "Out!"

The two looked at each other and paused.

Hardy saw their hesitation and said coldly, "You heard the man. Now climb out of that buggy or get shot where you are."

They glanced at each other again and then, reluctantly, both awkwardly climbed down on Hardy's side.

"That's better," he said, grinning. Then he turned and asked, "Which one, Charlie?"

Quinn pointed to the first tree, the one overlooking the huge boulders. "That one," he said. "Those rocks are tall enough you don't even have to sit 'em on a horse to get the job done."

Jerry said, "You're going to hang us!"

"Hey, Charlie, he really is a lawyer, ain't he?"

Jill shouted at them, "You bastards!"

"Listen, Quinn," Jerry said excitedly. "You don't want to hang Jill! She's still Farnsworth's daughter. He's part of your Combine. You *can't* hang her!"

Hardy grinned and said to Quinn, "He hasn't heard the latest news, has he, Charlie?"

Jerry glanced at Hardy and then asked, "What's he talking about?"

Quinn replied calmly, "It seems that your girlfriend over there is no longer Daddy's favorite. And that means that all bets are off and he agreed to the hangin'." Then the two noticed the chilling look in Quinn's eyes when he said tautly, "Parents are a bitch, aren't they?"

Both of them didn't know where that remark was coming from, but the revelation that Jill's own father would approve of her murder was startling enough.

Quinn said gravely, "All right, Counselor. You've addressed the jury and we're not swayed." Then his eyes went to Hardy and he nodded.

Hardy and the men pulled the struggling pair over to the boulders beneath the cottonwood. Two other men had already fashioned nooses from their own saddle ropes and expertly threw them over the highest, sturdiest branch directly overhanging the boulders. Jill tried to kick the cowboys in the ankles with her boot heels and they cried out when she made contact.

"Damn bitch!" one man cried.

"Don't worry, Vic," said Quinn evenly. "She'll be dancin' on air in a minute." Casually, he took out the makings and started to roll a cigarette. Cupping his hands, he lit it and blew out some smoke. Idly, he noticed there was a slight breeze blowing from the east and wondered if a storm might be kicking up.

Awkwardly, their captors pulled the two young people up atop the two tallest boulders and, holding them down, clumsily tried to drape the nooses around their necks. Both of them kept moving their heads to avoid the ropes, but the men who held them weren't gentle about how they did their jobs. One man grabbed a fistful of Jill's hair and yanked her head back. She cried out but was helpless to do anything about it. As the rope was pulled down on her face, its rough surface scraped against her eyes and nose before it finally settled around her neck. Then the man pulled the noose taut, causing her to gasp and choke audibly.

Jerry tried to kick the men holding him, but they dodged his feet and, after a few moments, were finally able to put the noose down around his neck. The two were then held in place atop the boulders as still another man reached up and tied the ends of both ropes firmly to the huge branch.

Quinn calmly looked up at them and took a drag from his cigarette. Hardy finally finished and got down off the boulders to stand next to him. Unlike Quinn, he was grinning from ear to ear.

Gazing at them coldly, Quinn decided to give them a speech. He knew it was BS, but it was all part of the game. Looking up at them, he announced, "You two murdered Ches Kinderstrom and have tried to assassinate the heads of our Combine. Your swingin' bodies will be a warnin' to all homesteaders not to rustle McDermott cattle."

Jerry would've roundly cursed at him, but the noose was already cutting off what little air he was getting. His eyes shifted to Jill worriedly; he hated to think how the rope was choking *her*.

Quinn's eyes went to the two men perched behind the boulders, ready to push the two off.

Then he looked at the doomed couple and said grimly, "If you make it to Heaven, say hello to the angels. But if you two are headin' south, give the devil my address."

He was about to give his men the signal to push them off until a gunshot sounded, and a bullet chipped the top of Jill's boulder.

Quinn dropped his cigarette and drew his gun. The men near the boulders ducked behind them and the others drew their guns and followed Quinn and Hardy as they ran into the covering shade of the cottonwoods.

Jerry and Jill heard the gunfire and their eyes scanned the hilltop. Yet they could only make out a vague silhouette of a man firing a handgun down at the group hiding in the trees.

As a bullet chipped the trunk of the tree he was hiding behind, Hardy cried, "Who the hell is it?"

"I don't know!" Quinn yelled back. "But the point of bein' all the way out here is so there's no witnesses!"

Then he stuck his head out and fired up at the hilltop.

The other men also fired up at the man on the hill, but it was useless to make out their target.

"Damn!" yelled Quinn. "Son of a bitch has got the sun behind 'em and he's too damn far anyway!"

Hardy cursed and fired at the upper rim of the hill.

"Save your ammo!" Quinn yelled to the men. "He's too far to hit and it's the same reason he can't hit us either—unless we give him a target!"

Hardy cringed behind a tree trunk and said, "Then he can't stop us!"

Quinn replied, "He can if he puts away that Colt and switches to a rifle. The horses are tied up behind us way back in the trees. By the time we get to our saddle boots and get our Winchesters, he could be circlin' around to get the jump on us."

"Damn, Charlie, he's got to be only one man."

"It only takes just one man to kill any of us." Then Quinn looked at the two people perched on the boulders and said, "But we could still get our work done." He cupped his hands and yelled, "Hey, Vic! Push 'em off!"

Vic got the message. He holstered his gun, then rose slightly and steadied himself against the top of Jill's boulder to push her off.

Seeing this, Jerry kicked out with his right foot, careful to keep his left foot on the rock and not uproot himself; with his hands tied behind his back and both his feet off the rock's surface, he'd be dangling and the noose would tighten around his neck in an instant.

At first, Vic ducked beneath Jerry's persistent kicks, but the New Yorker's leg was still long enough to prevent him from reaching Jill.

Then, to Jerry's surprise, Jill turned around and kicked the gunman full in the chest with the sharp toe of her boot. Vic grunted painfully and fell back behind the boulder.

Quinn saw this and cursed. Then he cried, "Johnny! Dusty! Push 'em off!"

With Vic writhing painfully on the ground, Johnny and Dusty were now the two men closest to the boulders. Ducking low to avoid the gunfire from the hill, they climbed the boulders and attempted to reach out and push them off.

Jerry quickly swung his foot out and the toe of his boot connected with Johnny's left eye. The gunman screamed and fell back, throwing a hand to his bleeding eye socket.

However, Jerry could not kick out at both of them and while

he was able to dispatch Johnny, Dusty was able to reach out and push Jill's feet off the top of the boulder. Immediately, her figure swung off into space and she started choking as she swayed back and forth.

Tears formed in Jerry's eyes as he stared at her helplessly. She was spaced too far apart on the branch for him to even reach out a foot to her.

Suddenly, rifle fire sounded from the hilltop. In fact, the barrage was so steady and deliberate, that Quinn curiously stuck his head out to see exactly where the man was firing. In a second, he realized what was happening. He watched, fascinated, as the rifle cartridges were chipping away at the weakest part of the branch that held the two young people.

Jerry saw this and quickly realized he had to aid the marksman on the hill by speeding up the breaking of the branch. Dismissing any thoughts of self-preservation, he jumped off the boulder. Almost immediately, the noose tightened around his throat and he began choking, but it had to be done to help save Jill.

In those few seconds, as he dangled in mid-air and his oxygen was being cut off, he had time for one quick thought: *Without her, it didn't matter anyway.*

Then, even as he started to pass out, he heard the cracking of wood and the branch dropped lower by several feet. Now their feet were about two feet off the ground.

Seeing this, Quinn cursed again and screamed, "Get him! Get that bastard on the hill!"

Several men, including Vic, rushed out into the open, more frightened by Charlie Quinn's rage than by the man on the hill. In a group, they fired up at the rim, but with the setting sun in their eyes, their bullets weren't going anywhere near their target.

The rifle fire continued without letup until one cartridge finally pierced a particularly stubborn piece of wood that held the branch together. Then a loud snap was heard and both Jerry and Jill loosely tumbled to the ground, their nooses still tied to the now fallen branch.

Now with his task out of the way, the man on the hill turned his attention to Vic and the other two men firing up at him. In rapid succession, he shot them down, with one cartridge piercing Dusty's throat and coming out the other side.

Quinn cursed yet again as he saw his men cut down so easily.

Despite his own rage, Hardy stared at the three dead men in wonder.

"Goddamn!" he said. "I *never* saw shootin' like that!"

The firing continued, the rifle slugs getting uncomfortably close to the trees.

Quinn said, "He must have a spare rifle."

Suddenly, rifle fire sprang from the hillside on the group's left.

"What the hell!"

Quinn said, "Bastard's got company!"

"What do we do now, Charlie?"

"We're prime targets down here, and we can't go out the way we came. Tell the others to get their horses and go back out through the trees. We'll swing around and head back to the ranch."

"We're not gonna stay and fight?"

"Not with that jasper on the hill hittin' everything in Creation he aims at."

"McDermott ain't gonna like this."

Quinn said irritably, "I don't give a damn whether he likes it or not. There weren't supposed to be any witnesses to the hangin's. Now we've got a whole hillside of witnesses and I'm not puttin' my own neck in a noose for Tad McDermott or anyone else! Come on!"

Firing their Colts up at the hill, they backed deeper into the trees as even more rifle fire erupted from more positions on the hillside. Jess Reid, the man whom Jerry buffaloed in town and still had a bandage tied around his head, turned around to run and was shot in the back.

Hidden in the underbrush, the crew, now consisting of just four men, including the two leaders, mounted their horses and rode back through an old Indian trail within the forest, to make it out the other side. They continued riding west until they were out of the area.

Lying on the dead grass with his hands still tied behind him, Jerry shook his head and then breathed deeply, gradually regaining his strength. Then he experimentally blinked his eyes and looked ahead of him. He saw Jill's figure a few feet away from him. Her hair was all over her face and her eyes were closed. He noticed that her mouth was wide open, but he didn't see her chest rise and fall beneath her brother's shirt.

He swallowed, trying to regain strength in his throat. Then he said thickly, "Jill? Jill?"

She didn't answer.

Awkwardly, he maneuvered his body even closer to her. Clumsily, getting to his knees, he hovered over her and gazed down at her lovely face, now absolutely still. Then he took a deep breath and leaned down on her, his open mouth covering hers. Ignoring his own labored breath, he pushed air as hard as he could into her open mouth. Then he raised himself slightly and took another deep breath. Again, he put his mouth on hers and pushed as much air into her as possible. He repeated the procedure another half dozen times before she suddenly started to cough.

Hovering over her, he smiled. Then he bent forward and again put his mouth on hers, just to make sure she got enough air into her lungs. As he did this, he became vaguely aware of people standing over him.

Jill's eyes opened then and the first thing she saw was Jerry's grateful smile. As she took in huge gulps of much-needed air, she smiled back, her eyes searching his face, seeing how glad he was to have her alive.

Then they both looked up at the people surrounding them, many of whom Jill instantly recognized as homesteaders. Then tears formed in her eyes as she saw that the one in the forefront of the group was her brother Morgan. He was carrying a rifle with smoke still curling out of the barrel.

Taking off his Stetson, Morgan ran his hand back through his hair and looked down at them.

Facing Jerry, he said mildly, "Now, listen, Bingham. I don't mind you sparkin' with my sister, but don't you think there's a better time and place?"

CHAPTER NINE

IT WAS DARK NOW.

Both Jerry and Jill were seated in separate chairs in the cabin of the Jabotinskys. They were holding mugs of hot coffee poured frequently by Mrs. Jabotinsky. Morgan and six other men were either seated or leaning against something. Most of their rifles had been piled in a corner.

Jill stared at her brother and shook his head.

"I just can't believe it," she said, grinning. "*You* shot that tree branch apart?"

Morgan said sardonically, "I cannot tell a lie. I did it with my little Winchester Seventy-six."

Jerry said, "Looks like all that target practice firing at bottles and cans paid off, huh?"

Morgan answered, "If it didn't, friend, you wouldn't be sitting there now and asking me."

Jerry lifted his mug to Morgan and said, "Touché, friend."

"I'm just glad I was able to pass the Cumberlands' place and let Sam know what was happening. Then he rode over to the Carson's, and they got to the Jabotinskys, and...well, we had enough numbers on McDermott's bunch to even things out a bit."

"But one thing puzzles me," Jerry said. "How did you know they were taking us somewhere to lynch us?"

"Bill Connors told me."

Jill stared at her brother and said, "Connors!"

Morgan nodded and said, "I'll admit, it sounds kinda strange to me too. Isn't he working with McDermott?"

Jerry gave a little half-smile and said, "It seems that Bill Connors is harder to figure out than a math equation."

"He told me about it, but he refused to come himself. Said he had to make it look like he had nothing to do with it."

Jerry nodded thoughtfully and said, "He's smart. If McDermott found out he helped us, they'd kill him. I strongly suspect *he's* the one who fired that rifle at McDermott's men while I was fighting with Hardy."

Jill shook her head, still not believing it all.

"I'll be damned," she said quietly. Then she remembered where she was. "I'm sorry, Missus Jabotinsky."

Mrs. Jabotinsky was a tall, thin woman in her thirties with slightly stooped shoulders from carrying buckets of milk on a landlord's farm back in St. Petersburg. With a slight wave of her calloused hand, she dismissed Jill's concern and said, "Don't worry about it, dear. Vladimir and I have heard Cossacks curse much worse than that."

After pouring more steaming coffee into Jerry's mug, she came over to Jill and held the pot out to her for a refill.

"Oh!" said Jill, with a tired smile. "Thank you, Missus Jabotinsky, but I've had enough for now. You've been too kind."

"Don't worry," Mrs. Jabotinsky said, "there's plenty more when you want it."

Due to so many people in his house and a lack of chairs for

them all, Vladimir Jabotinsky was seated on a packing crate in a corner of the sparse room, lighting his pipe. He was a tall, bearded man who always wore a cap, even indoors. Besides his wide shoulders, his arms were deceptively muscular and his legs strong. In the old country, he had spent much of his time outdoors, whether it was hot or bitterly cold, literally doing the work of two plow horses, all so that he and his wife could barely have enough to eat.

He said drily, "Rifke, the young lady said she doesn't want any more. Leave her be."

Mrs. Jabotinsky turned back and replied, "Yes, Vladimir, I heard her. But *you* try living through a lynching."

Jabotinsky puffed on his pipe and said, "A lynching? No, can't say I've seen one of those. But when I was a boy, I've survived a pogrom or two." His eyes were small and far away, remembering. Then he faced Jerry across the room and said, "What you two went through happens every day to us in Russia and Poland and the Middle East. Rifke and I still can't believe it can happen here in this country. And the funny thing is, it's not because of your religion either."

"No," said Jerry pensively, "it's because of the fact that we're the thorns in the side of a very ruthless—and probably very insane —man."

Sam Cumberland was leaning against the log walls, his rifle still at his side. He was a tall, rangy man with receding hair the color of straw and piercing gray eyes. He cuffed his beaten-up Stetson back on his head and said, "Now you see what we've been dealing with for the past year, Bingham. McDermott and his crew have been murdering us right, left and in-between, but even his fifty killers can't murder us that fast. The more they wipe out families and burn homesteads, the more new arrivals keep coming in. They're from the east, or the south, or, like the Jabotinskys here, Eastern Europe. Tad McDermott can't stop the Homestead

Act and the folks in Washington and in Omaha won't kill the bill to satisfy a bunch of grasping thieves with their own private terrorist army. But they're also not sending anyone to protect us either. We're in the wilderness and the federals are too damn far away from us to care."

Everyone was silent for a while, going over what Cumberland had just said.

Pete Hamlin was sitting on an old stool and had a toothpick in his mouth. Abruptly, he clapped his huge hands together and said, "Seems pretty simple to me, folks. When the world doesn't care what happens to us, we've got to do whatever we can to defend ourselves. And if the world starts squawkin' about it, to hell with 'em!"

They parted shortly afterward, but they all decided to meet again the next day and plan strategy.

The homesteaders had captured the buggy and two horses near the lynching site and, with a full moon above them, Morgan was now at the reins driving it back to their place. Both Jerry and Jill were squeezed together beside him in the seat. Their clothes were torn and caked with dust and their tired muscles ached even more in the cramped seats.

Pushed close to Jill, Jerry had his arm around her shoulders. He looked down at her then. Her head was against his chest and the only sounds they heard was the soft rhythmic clip-clop of the horses trotting down the trail. She appeared to be dozing and he watched with interest as her chest rose and fell as she slept. If he moved his arm, he was afraid he might wake her; but he also realized that he liked having his arm around her anyway.

As he watched her, he immediately saw the deep red circle about her throat. He experimentally touched his own neck with his free hand and felt the indentation made from the noose. He hadn't had a chance to look at himself in a mirror, but the gash must be as dark and ugly as hers. Considering the psychological pressures that both he and Jill had suffered throughout this range war, he bitterly reflected that they were now physically scarred by it as well.

Keeping his voice low, Morgan asked, "She asleep?"

Jerry turned his head only slightly so as not to wake Jill.

"Yes, she is," he said.

"Poor girl. She's suffered more than anyone 'cause of this whole mess. She hasn't got a father. And thanks to my drinkin' and all-around melancholy, she didn't have much of a brother either for a while."

Jerry said earnestly, "Well, she got him back tonight."

Morgan glanced at him, then faced the trail ahead.

"Thanks," he said, "but my sister doesn't need an albatross around her neck like me."

"You're not an albatross, Morg."

"I *am*. A little over a year ago the army needed more scouts for the campaign to capture Dull Knife and his band. Well, Emma Lou and I weren't exactly drowning in money and splendor in our tiny cabin, so I figured we could use the extra pay I'd get from the army. So, I went away for a few months. When I returned—" His voice cracked for a moment and Jerry saw how hard it was for him to continue.

He said gently, "You don't have to go any further."

"No," said Morgan firmly. "I've *got* to tell it. I've kept it cooped up inside me for too long...So...when I got back, there she was hanging from that tree that's not there anymore, with a Tad McDermott noose around her neck." He looked at Jerry earnestly. "When I saw my sister about to die the same way Emma Lou did... I tell you, Bingham, something exploded in me. My vision shook and I couldn't see straight."

Jerry said quietly, "You saw straight enough, my friend, and for that I'm eternally grateful."

Morgan shook his head and said, "Lord, I *never* fired a gun like that before! But when I looked at that tree branch, even in the fading light, I made out every detail of that thing as if it were two inches in front of me rather than a hundred yards." Glancing at Jill, he asked, "She still asleep?"

Jerry glanced at her and said, "Um-hm."

Morgan said earnestly, "You know, Bingham, she likes you. She can't stop talking about you at home."

Suddenly, Jill shifted in her seat and buried her head even deeper into Jerry's chest.

Morgan continued, "My stepfather would've had our place burned to the ground if not for her staying there to keep me company. Guess she was also afraid I'd shoot myself after Emma Lou died." He paused for a moment, then added, "She needs a good man, Bingham. Someone to take her far way from this madness."

"Jill might have her own ideas about that."

Morgan nodded and said, "True enough. But at least you two have faced something together she'll never face with another man."

"Yeah? What's that?"

With his eyes still on the trail, he said quietly, "Death…"

They *had* to stop somewhere and rest.

They had fled with their tails between their legs and they knew it. One jasper on a hill had outgunned them, and if that weren't bad enough, some of his friends had shown up and ended the show.

They had stopped and camped about ten miles from the vast McDermott spread, in a hollow with a group of low hills on one side and a smattering of cottonwoods on the other; this was done in order to obscure the view of any drifter or enemy who happened to be riding by. To whoever was left of the group that started out, it was a move marked by desperation as well as caution.

The men were not happy about Charlie Quinn's order to have cold camp, but the McDermott ramrod was not taking any chances. He didn't know whether the group back at the hanging site was pursuing them, so the less light from a campfire the better; as it was, the moon was shimmering brightly enough for any halfway good tracker to see in. His men were tired, hungry and fed up. For the first time in its months' long existence, McDermott's crew was on the run, and no amount of whiskey or other false reassurance was going to change that fact.

Quinn was leaning on the trunk of a lone cottonwood, lighting yet another cigarette. He exhaled a mouthful into his lungs and let it out slowly. His eyes seemed empty as he stared at nothing in particular. Hardy silently approached him. The others knew that when Charlie was like this, Hardy was the *only* one who could approach him.

Somewhere among the men, sprawled on the ground with their quickly rolled cigarettes and their surreptitious swigs from flasks of whiskey, was the wounded Johnny Daves with a rag over his bleeding left eye. During their ignoble retreat, two men had helped him up on his horse and they had all ridden out, with the wounded man yelling in agony all the way. Now that they were all settled down in camp, he was still yelling—and it was grating on the nerves.

Ignoring Johnny's yowls of pain, Hardy said quietly, "The men are out of it, Charlie. Right now, you couldn't get 'em to attack a women's sewin' circle."

Quinn said wryly, "And they'd probably lose anyway..."

"What the hell happened back there, Charlie?"

Quinn looked at him for the first time and his eyes lost their hollow gaze, replaced instead by rage.

"What happened?" he repeated. "We were outgunned and outfought, *that's* what happened. When they threw equal numbers at us, albeit firin' from concealed positions, they were able to take us, and take us good." Then he stared at the ground and said, "What gets my goat is, who told them. *Who told them!* I was the only man alive to read that note sent by McDermott. It was sealed in an envelope, I had to cut it open! The courier couldn't have seen it, and no one knew what we were goin' to do, but the boss. Couldn't be any other way, it was a rush job. There was *no time* for anyone to know about it."

"Someone else could've known," ventured Hardy. "That bunch of self-important high-hats who kiss the boss' boots. Tad might've told them what he was gonna do."

Quinn shook his head, deep in thought. "I don't know," he said. "One thing's for sure. *Somebody* talked. And if I ever find the man, I'll see his insides, I swear."

"You and me both, friend."

Quinn glanced at the men and asked, "Lickin' their wounds, eh?"

Hardy replied, "They'll get over it. They're tough boys, Charlie."

"Yeah," said Quinn cynically, "they're tough while they have the numbers on their sides, just like the Indians. But we lost some men tonight. In fact, we've been knocked down to size ever since Bingham came here and teamed up with that Carmody bitch." He cursed and tossed away his quirley. "Damn! We could've ended a lot of this mess had we been allowed to finish the job back there."

"That's an idea."

"What is?"

"That Carmody girl. Maybe her old man had a change of heart and decided not to let us hang his daughter. You know, he told McDermott one thing, then double-crossed him and let a bunch of settlers know what we were plannin'. Then they trailed us to the hangin' and let us have it."

Quinn stared at him.

"Maybe you've got somethin' there, Al."

"'Course I do. *Who else* would've blabbed?"

Quinn was about to say something else but was interrupted by loud cries coming from behind Hardy. Johnny staggered around him and faced Quinn. His left hand was pushing a blood-soaked rag against his eye.

He whined, "I need a doctor!"

Hardy looked at him and said, "There ain't one around, so shut up."

Johnny cried out, "I fought for you, Quinn, and all I got for it is the loss of my eye! Damn it! Aren't you going to do anything for me! What about my eye, damn it! What about my eye?!"

Quinn quickly drew his gun and shot Johnny, who screamed and fell heavily to the ground.

Looking down at his body, Hardy said, "Now you've got no eyes at all!"

Holstering his smoking gun, Quinn said, "Can't stand whiners."

"Neither can I."

Behind them, the men stared at the scene; some of them taking an extra snort of whiskey.

They were gathered inside Pete Hamlin's cabin, which was barely larger than the Jabotinskys'. Hamlin wasn't serving coffee; his house wasn't usually open for guests and he just had provisions for himself. His wife had died during childbirth, as had his son, and ever since then, few had ever set foot inside the cabin for social calls.

Vladimir Jabotinsky stood by the open window, staring at the rangeland beyond, his Winchester at his side in case an attack should come from that direction. Jill sat beside Jerry in a moth-eaten couch with a used saddle blanket for a cover. Back at the Carmodys' cabin, she had slept deeply in her room while Jerry slept on an extra cot in Morgan's room.

After they arrived at the Carmodys' cabin the night before, Morgan had put the confiscated horses and buggy in their barn. He then unhitched the two horses and fed and watered them, putting them in stalls next to his own mount. McDermott's crew had stolen their own horses, so Morgan bequeathed the captured animals to Jerry and Jill.

"We all here?" asked Cumberland.

"No one else is coming," said Jabotinsky, gazing through the window.

Pete Hamlin remarked, "Folks are scared."

"Can you blame them?" Jabotinsky asked.

"Guess not."

There were twenty people in the room, including Jerry and the Carmody siblings.

Suddenly, Jabotinsky stiffened at the window and readied his rifle.

"Rider coming."

Cumberland got up from the thick wooden barrel he was sitting on and went over to the window. Standing beside Jabotinsky, he asked, "If he doesn't look familiar, let 'em have it."

Jabotinsky looked at him and said wryly, "Not until I see the whites of his eyes, my friend."

Cumberland grunted.

The rider finally rode over to the tie rail, dismounted and

wrapped the reins around it. It was young Hank Austin. His folks had traveled all the way from Kansas after their property was burned by Quantrill's Bushwhackers, and then were promptly murdered by McDermott's crew right after they built their cabin. Austin had been staying with classmate Laurie Macklin and her folks at the other end of the valley.

Hank ran up to the door and went right in, a rolled-up newspaper in his hand. Right after he closed the door, he announced, "Mornin', all! Sorry I'm late. While I was in town, I picked this up."

Jerry said to the group, "*He's* joining us? Isn't he a little young?"

Cumberland said gruffly, "They murdered his folks and took his land. He's old enough."

Jerry absorbed this and sat back, humbled.

Jill leaned over and said quietly, "Out here, youngins start totin' guns when they're twelve."

Jerry sarcastically replied, "Why wait till they're that old?"

Hank went over to Jerry and handed him the newspaper.

"Here you go, Bingham. You'll be real interested in this."

"What is it?"

"Look."

Jerry opened the paper and he and Jill read the headline. There it was in bold capital letters:

Two Rustlers Hanged By Vengeful Cattlemen!

JERRY READ the article out loud. "'The other day, the territory's cattlemen, fed up with the outrageous string of cattle rustling, have said enough is enough!!!'" He looked up and said, "There are actually *three* exclamation points at the end of this sentence. What responsible journalist would actually write like that?"

"Keep readin', Bingham," said Curtis Rogers. He was a former Texas cowboy who rode the herds up to Abilene for twenty-two years. The open ranges of western Nebraska gave him and his family a chance to start a ranch of their own. Quinn's men murdering two of his sons while they were minding their father's newly bought cattle brought an edge to his personality. If Rogers was not a man who freely expressed his emotions before, the murders of his sons had now made him harder than stone.

Jerry continued. "Jerry Bingham, the son of that no-good bandit, George Bingham—" He was getting angry just reading it and would have stopped, but Jill gently squeezed his arm, letting him know that she was there. He looked at her beautiful eyes for a moment, then read on.

"...That no-good bandit, George Bingham, and his...his..." He looked up at Jill again.

She said quietly, "It's all right, Jerry. I can guess what they said about me."

"I don't want to read any more."

Jill took the paper and read it out loud. "...his...his fallen woman, Jill Carmody, the stepsister of outlaw Morgan Carmody."

Seated on a box on the other side of the stove, Morgan said cheerfully, "Hah! Outlaw! I like that!"

She continued, "These two heinous felons have been the leaders of the most murderous band of cutthroats ever to ride the range. They have stolen cattle, burned property and threatened to assassinate the cattlemen if they continued to fight them. They are responsible for the murder of *Sentinel* editor Ches Kinderstrom, whose body was found in Pawnee Creek with water flowing all around it...In all honesty, how could anyone blame the cattlemen and their loyal crews when they take matters into their own hands and dispense some much-needed range justice so long denied."

Jill angrily crumpled the newspaper in her fist and said, "Such filth. What'd you think they'd say?"

Pete Hamlin said, "How do you two folks feel now that the Sentinel has declared you dead?"

Jerry answered, "Very, very angry."

"Good," replied Hamlin. "We're gonna need that anger."

Now was the time, they all decided, to hit at McDermott and his crew while they were at their weakest. They had suffered the loss of several men; there didn't seem to be a better opportunity.

"Before," said Cumberland, "we were just a bunch of home-steaders spread all over miles of countryside, separated by distance and..." His eyes went to Jabotinsky then. "...And maybe separated by culture as well...But I think we've had more than we can take. The last straw was when they tried to hang those two young folks. So, I say, it's time to teach these fanatics a lesson."

One of the men sitting on the floor near the stove was a little man named John Bright. He looked up at Cumberland and absently nodded. However, even as he idly sat there, sallow and poker-faced, he took in everything that was said, and made mental notes of every aspect of their plans.

When the combine met again in Tad McDermott's living room, the other cattlemen avoided Eugene Farnsworth's eyes. They had conspired to murder his daughter and, consequently, they just couldn't bear to look at the man.

Bennett was serving them all tea and cake, though all of them opted for the bottle of brandy that the butler brought to them in case anyone wanted anything stronger than tea.

An added incentive for the brandy was the presence of Charlie Quinn, who was standing near the entrance to the foyer, hatless, but not unarmed. The others were clearly scared of him and they had a tough time trying to act as if he wasn't there; his narrowed eyes were watching every move they made.

Seated in his usual cushioned chair under the portrait of the great Scottish warrior, Tad McDermott puffed on a cigar and stared at his partners, of whom he had only the greatest contempt. Len Cagle sat in a separate chair on the other side of the room and was drinking a cup of tea, his eyes taking in the sight of the other men with disdain.

"I'm sure," Cagle began, "you've all heard by now of our failure to rid this countryside of our two worst pains in the ass."

Judge Alcott said, "I don't understand it. How'd the settlers find out what you were going to do?"

"Somebody talked," said Quinn bluntly. All heads turned to him and none of the cattle barons except McDermott could look at Quinn's eyes for very long. To those four men, there was something behind those black eyes which was just not normal.

"But *who?*" the judge asked.

McDermott leaned forward and stared across the room at Eugene Farnsworth. "Yes," said McDermott tensely. "Who, indeed?"

The look chilled Farnsworth and he almost dropped his full glass of brandy.

"W-why are you looking at me?" he asked.

McDermott said through his teeth, "Because you're so *clever,* Gene, that's why."

"Why, what—"

"I'll tell you why, Gene! Because it looks like blood *is* thicker than water around here, that's why!"

At this point, Farnsworth was shaking so hard, his brandy was spilling all over McDermott's nice red carpet. He quickly put the glass down on the table before him.

"But, but I didn't say anything!"

McDermott's eyes became slits. He said harshly, "You didn't, huh? You knew what we were going to do to your daughter. I said, 'She dies,' and you agreed to it. You *agreed* to it, damn it!" His fist hit the coffee table before him, and the sharp bang made the four cattle barons jump. Quinn just idly gazed at his boss and Cagle smirked.

"No one lies to me, Gene, ya hear me, *no one!*"

Farnsworth was openly sweating now, and his hands were shaking. Had both of the women he married and later murdered been alive to see it, they would've had a time trying to suppress their glee at his suffering.

Farnsworth stammered, "B-but I *didn't* know! You just said you were going to frame them for Kindersun—"

"Kinder*strom*," corrected Judge Alcott.

Farnsworth shouted, "Oh, shut up, you stupid old man!"

The judge stared at him, open-mouthed.

The accused man then faced McDermott and said, "But I swear, Tad! You said you were going to frame Bingham and my daughter—"

McDermott said, "*Your daughter*, huh? The one you said you disowned."

"Hell, Tad, I don't want any part of her! You saw her slap my face."

"In my opinion, she didn't slap it hard enough."

The others laughed then, all except Charlie Quinn, who just gazed at the accused man without expression; and Tad McDermott, who glared at him with barely concealed rage. As Farnsworth looked helplessly around the room at the other cattle barons, he saw them for what they were: Dressed-up animals who were clearly enjoying someone else's misery. They were also obviously glad that Tad McDermott's rage was not directed at any of *them*.

"I'm telling you!" Farnsworth shouted. "You were going to use the Swede's murder as a pretext to hang them, but I didn't talk!"

McDermott gestured towards the others and said, "Well, one of you men talked, and quite frankly I don't think these three men are *that* stupid, do you?"

Suddenly, a realization hit Judge Alcott like a flash of lightening and his face turned white. He quickly downed the glass of brandy in his hand and hoped it would bring some much-needed color back to his face and settle his morbid fear of what would happen to him if McDermott found out the truth.

McDermott pointed with his cigar and said, "You're the only man here with a good reason to tell the homesteaders the whole plan. That goddamn bitch of a daughter you sired!" Then his voice sounded as rough as sandpaper scraping against wood. "*No one* stops my plans, Gene, and lives to tell about it..."

The look on McDermott's hard face was too much for Farnsworth. In a burst of animal fear, he sprang from his chair and ran past Charlie Quinn into the foyer. He got to the front door and had just enough time to pull it open before Quinn drew his gun and shot him in the back.

Farnsworth stiffened with the shot and fell forward, the weight of his body shutting the door as he slid down to the carpeted floor.

McDermott rose and stared into the foyer. He shouted, "Bennett!"

The butler quickly appeared and stood attentively under the archway.

"Sir?"

McDermott gestured at the body with his cigar.

Bennett went into the foyer. He lifted Farnsworth up into his arms and was about to drag him away until there was a knock on the door. Bennett quickly dropped him and went to the door.

He opened it just a little and said, "Yes?"

After a pause, Bennett opened the door all the way and let in John Bright. However, when the little man looked down and saw Farnsworth lying on the floor, he gave a sharp cry.

"Oh, stop it, Bright," said McDermott irritably. "Just come in already."

Trying vainly to suppress his fear, Bright gingerly stepped over Farnsworth and entered the living room, hat in hand. He stared at all of them and noticed that three of the cattle barons were white and shaken, compulsively drinking brandy as if it had gone out of style. Len Cagle was staring back at him, totally unperturbed by the sight of a dead body in the foyer, and Quinn was openly glaring at the little man as if he were a tick annoying his horse, Fred.

Meanwhile, Bennett continued dragging Farnsworth away. Bright couldn't help staring at the butler as he went about his work.

McDermott gruffly shouted, "We're *over here*, Bright! Now I'm payin' you goddamn enough, what the hell do you have to report?"

The voice shook him, and he faced McDermott, swallowing nervously as he did so.

"Well," he began, "you were right about the settlers. They're planning on hitting you and your crew."

"Is that so? When?"

"Day after tomorrow."

"Where?"

"Mister Ridgeway's place, the Flying R Ranch."

Ridgeway sat forward, belching before he spoke.

"Excuse me. *My* ranch? But why?"

McDermott said, "Because you're one of the Combine, that's why. What else?"

Bright answered, "We're supposed to meet at the foot of Kelton Hill at ten o'clock in the morning day after tomorrow and then ride over to the Flying R and take their horses."

"That's it?" said McDermott. "Just take their horses?"

Bright was still nervous and paused before speaking. He felt Charlie Quinn glaring at him and was fighting the temptation to relieve himself in front of the whole roomful of people as he stood there.

"*Today*, man!" McDermott shouted.

"Yes!" said Bright, reluctantly continuing. "They said Mister Ridgeway's ranch was going to be the first place they'd hit. Then they'd hit all the other ranches in the Combine, stealing their horseflesh and locking them up somewhere. Sam Cumberland said this would..." He shut his eyes trying to remember the phrase he used. "He said...he said it would 'kill your mobility'. He said if they took all the horses, you couldn't ride out after them, and then they'd 'catch you cold', was how he put it." Bright nodded affirmatively at his own recitation and grinned for the first time.

McDermott said gruffly, "It's still a stupid plan. They should be goin' after *us*, not our animals."

"Not necessarily," said Quinn. "Maybe they don't have the stomach for fightin' us to the death, so they're hittin' our ability to move. Then they figure to capture us while we're standin' still. It's easy to run our horses off; they just have to attack the ranches and fire into the air; those animals will head for the hills right quick."

Len Cagle said, "He's right, Tad. Break our ability to move and strike quickly and the crew won't be able to accomplish its function to drive everyone out of the valley."

McDermott rubbed his chin and scowled. His three partners

were still too shaken up by the second shooting in front of them in the past three days to make any comments.

"All right," McDermott finally said, pointing with his cigar, "this is what we do. Charlie, you get the boys together and hit the Cumberland place tomorrow mornin'—*a day before* they're supposed to hit us. Then have another crew hit the Carmody place at the same time."

Quinn said, "I'd love to, Mister McDermott, but there's one problem."

"What's that?"

"During the past few days, for one reason or another, our men have been steadily killed off." He didn't bother to mention his own killing of Vic Frawley and Al Hardy's pistol-whipping of Phil Devery. He said, "Our numbers are down, and we need the sheer volume of men to split off into squads of ten or more in order to overpower the homesteaders. To hit both the Cumberland and the Carmodys' at the same time would stretch us to the limit if the settlers are organizin'."

McDermott thought about this. After a moment, he looked at the three partners on the couch and said, "Gentlemen, you're ridin' with us."

The three men stared at him in shock.

Ridgeway whined, "But we're not gunmen."

"No," said Len Cagle wryly, "you just profit from their deeds."

Judge Alcott said, "Please, Tad! I've got a weak heart!"

McDermott said, "Some hard time in the saddle ridin' and killin' will give you strength, Judge." He leaned forward then, his eyes burning into the three men. "Then," he said quietly, "you'll be just like me. You'll learn to fear nothin'..."

CHAPTER TEN

TAD MCDERMOTT HAD A SPECIAL TASK FOR BENNETT TO PERFORM.

As they were leaving, McDermott's three surviving partners were forced to watch Bennett, now attired in a long black coat and Stetson, tie Eugene Farnsworth onto the back of a horse. Then the butler, riding a beautiful Palomino, pulled the reins of the second horse containing Farnsworth out onto the prairie and headed in a southeasterly direction.

Ridgeway saw the man riding away and took a long pull on his hip flask before climbing into his buggy for the ride back to the Flying R. Judge Alcott was mopping the sweat off his forehead and praying that McDermott would never find out that it was *he* who spilled the beans about the near-lynching. Honus Wilder just stared at the scene, never once forgetting that he and his partners had personally witnessed their senior partner and his chief hench-man, in separate incidents, shoot down two men in cold blood right before their horrified eyes.

It was almost enough to make one go back and face a prison back east, as they all rightfully should have.

Bennett had taken the long way around to get to the Carmody ranch, avoiding the indignity of having to duck and shrink under persistent, low-hanging tree branches on narrow Indian trails; it added another half hour to his journey, but it was worth it. Extremely loyal to Tad McDermott, he was the one who literally knew all-too well where the bodies were buried. Besides being the boss' expert part-time undertaker, he also felt that he was still a "gentleman's gentleman", and he balked at the inconvenience of squeezing his dignified, well-dressed frame through thick underbrush.

He appeared now about a hundred feet from the rear of the Carmody cabin. He skirted the trees at the back, quietly noting the one tree-stump among the group, and then pulled the rope that held Farnsworth to the back of the second mount. One pull on the rope and the knot came apart, unceremoniously dropping Farnsworth loosely to the ground.

After he fell, Bennett was in the act of turning his horse back towards the trail when he heard running footsteps in the soft earth back of the house.

Morgan had been getting some rest, and when he appeared, he was clad in his jeans and long underwear. In his bare feet, he ran across the backyard, a Winchester in his hands.

Without thinking, Bennett drew his pistol and instantly realized he had made a fatal mistake. Morgan quickly raised the rifle to his shoulder and fired.

The bullet hit the gentleman's gentleman firmly in the chest and he toppled from his horse, hitting the soft earth in a cloud of dust. Both horses, spooked by the gunshot and with no human hand to guide them, moved quickly away from the Carmody property, only to stop and drift around the low hills ringing the area.

Keeping his rifle at the ready, Morgan ran over to the spot and looked down at the two bodies. With his bare foot, he kicked away Bennett's Colt and then bent over to turn his body face up. He had never seen Bennett before, but quickly surmised that he must be one of McDermott's lackeys.   However, when he turned over his stepfather, his face stiffened.   Grimly, Morgan squatted down and put his hand on the old man's wrist.   He paused for just a moment before he slid his hands under his stepfather's body and lifted him up over his shoulders.   Awkwardly, with the old man's weight around his strong shoulders, Morgan then rose to his full height.

Suddenly, he heard footsteps running behind him and saw Jerry and Jill, both brandishing rifles, running up to him.   When Jill saw the face of the man her brother was carrying, she gasped.

Her eyes bore into his with a silent, but urgent question.

Reading her look, Morgan said, "No, Sis, I didn't shoot him." Then, as he marched towards the house with his burden, he added wryly, "Though I wish I had..."

Jill asked, "Well, if he's dead, why are you taking him into the house?"

Morgan stopped and turned around.

He replied gravely, "Because, big sister, our dear father happens to be alive..."

Perhaps it was because Quinn had shot the man in the shadows of the small foyer, or perhaps it was because he was forced to draw and fire in a split second and didn't have time to aim properly; but either way it looked, Quinn's bullet had merely skimmed the man's side and taken off a piece of skin, harmlessly bypassing any vital muscles or arteries.

Without thinking twice, the Carmodys and Jerry went to work with boiling water and clean cloth; when they could, draining the broken skin of pus, cleaning the wound with a bottle of whiskey, and then tightly tying a clean white sheet around the man's midsection. As the siblings were doing this, Jerry watched their faces, trying to gauge what they were thinking as they helped patch up the father who had betrayed them; but he could read nothing. Their faces were as impassive as stone.

They took shifts through the night, resting intermittently, and then waking up and going back out to the kitchen table to keep watch on the old man.

As he writhed on the wooden table, there were moments when he called out the names of his wives, and in his delirium, admitted that he loved them both, and feared them as well. At one point, all three of them were present when Farnsworth cried out how sorry he was that he had murdered them. Jerry watched the Carmodys and saw the tears roll down Jill's cheeks and Morgan's eyes grow moist as they gazed at their sorry excuse for a father.

Jerry noted that the siblings tried to ignore the old man's admission and talked about other things; the near-lynching, Morgan's expert shooting, Bill Connors informing Morgan of the lynching and indirectly saving their lives; they spoke of everything but the ugly things they had just heard from their father.

By early morning the next day, all three were confident enough to leave the old man alone and get some much-needed sleep. In fact, they were all sleeping so deeply that no one was around when Farnsworth's eyes fluttered open and he experimentally sat up on the table. He breathed fitfully, grateful to get some fresh air into his lungs. Then his eyes went down to his torso and he saw the bandage, with the area around his right side already crimson with dried blood.

Gradually, sunlight filtered through the window and it allowed him to gaze around the kitchen. He instantly recognized where he was, the cabin owned by his own children. Looking again at the bandage, tears came to his eyes and he almost wept unashamedly; but just as quickly, he shook off the emotion.

Farnsworth saw his bloody shirt and suit coat hung over a chair in the corner of the room. They were a mess, but they seemed to be the only clothes he could wear, at the moment.

Slowly, he rose off the table, figuring that they were asleep after a hard night of looking after him. He was already wearing his trousers and boots, so all he had to do was dress in his shirt and coat; which he did so carefully. His eyes scanned the hallway which led to the bedrooms and, satisfied that he had not awakened them, he left the kitchen, opened the front door and walked out of the house.

Then he quietly walked over to the barn, remembering that Morgan had also used it as a part-time tool shed. As he hobbled over to the barn door, he reflected that he had faced death, and quickly realized that it had imbued him with a renewed sense of purpose; he was now driven to do something he had never attempted before. And he knew that his rebirth was all thanks to the children he had turned against.

He was certain that somewhere in that barn he would find something there that would serve his newborn sense of purpose.

They were in such a deep sleep that they didn't hear the horse and buggy leave the property and head in the direction of Starrett City.

In fact, they didn't find out about it until four hours later. Jill was the first one to enter the kitchen, wipe the sleep from her eyes and see that the old man was gone.

She started at the sight and shouted, "Jerry! Morgan! Come out here!"

The two emerged groggily from Morgan's room and saw what Jill saw.

"My God!" said Jerry.

Jill ordered, "Search the place! He couldn't have gone too far."

They did so, searching everywhere around the property; but when Morgan returned from the barn, he told them.

Jill said, "What!"

Morgan said, "I'm afraid we did our job too well. He got up while we were sleeping and he lit out. He took one of the horses that dead man was riding and hooked him up to the buggy. And not only that, he took a few sticks of dynamite I was using to clear a patch of land for irrigation."

Jill asked, "But where the hell did he go?"

"There's no two ways about it. The tracks lead to town."

Jill's excitement grew. "Well, we've got to find him! He could be dying out there!"

Morgan put his hands on her shoulders and looked at her steadily.

"Listen to me, Sis! And listen good. We are in the middle of a damn range war and we're sitting targets."

"Yes, but—"

"I said, *listen*! We've got some things to do to protect ourselves and our land. We found that son of a bitch bleeding to death and we did the right thing. We didn't put a knife in him while he was sleeping, despite what he did to our moms. We patched him up and said, 'Live and let live.' Obviously, he didn't feel the need to stay around and thank us, and you know something? The hell with 'em! We've got our neighbors depending on us, so I'm not searching the territory for his sorry butt. If he's strong enough to drive a horse and buggy and go on a joy ride, then we can afford to find him when this whole thing is over."

Jerry said, "He's right, Jill. This is bigger than your father."

Jill paused and looked at both of them.

Quietly, she said, "All right, Morg. Let's get those bastards..."

After they ate breakfast, they mounted their horses and headed out. All of them had rifles in their saddle boots, and now even Jerry had a holstered gun strapped around his hips. Seeing that Jerry was not familiar with it, Morgan helped him tie the holster cord around his thigh so the pistol wouldn't bounce painfully against his leg as he rode.

Jerry felt strange now that he was wearing a hog leg. Having his usual New York-bought pistol in a shoulder holster was one thing; a man couldn't wear a gun out in the open in New York City as he could here in the west.

But this was indeed a long way from Fifth Avenue...

At 10 a.m., they were all sitting their horses at the foot of Kelton Hill, twenty-five strong.

Cumberland walked his horse over next to Jabotinsky. The Russian was sitting his horse and rolling a cigarette. After he cupped the match-flame against the valley wind and shook it out, he inhaled deeply and then blew out smoke into the crisp morning air.

Cumberland said wryly, "You think our friend John Bright will be pissed off when he finds out we double-crossed him and showed up here a day earlier?"

Jabotinsky turned and looked at him through a haze of rising smoke.

"No, my friend. But I have a feeling he'll end up in much worse shape before long..."

"I'm glad you acted on your suspicions and trailed him the other day to McDermott's ranch. What made you think he was a stooge for the Combine?"

Jabotinsky looked out at the valley and said quietly, "One reason was the fact that his one hundred-sixty acres was south of Pete Hamlin's place, where we held all our meetings. But every time he said he was headed back home, he rode west—which happens to be the same direction as McDermott's spread. Another is that he was always curious about infinitesimal details about our plans, but he never contributed anything in return. He had no ideas, no comments, no anything. He didn't give advice, he just kept asking us where, when and how—like he was going to repeat it to someone else. So, I followed him just to make sure..."

Cumberland looked at him oddly and said, "That word you used. Infinit..."

"Don't worry about it, Sam. We've got bigger things to think about besides grammar..."

All heads turned east when they spotted the three horses headed their way.

Curtis Rogers said, "I don't like it, Sam. You sure you want a woman ridin' with us?"

Cumberland looked across the group at the old Texan as he sat his horse. "Jill Carmody's got more sand than a lot of men," he said. "Maybe she's not Calamity Jane, but she'll do an awful lot of damage. Anyways, remember, McDermott's bunch tried to hang her and Bingham. She's got a score to settle, and frankly, I don't think I have a right to keep her out."

Rogers just grunted in reply.

After the three rode up to them, Jerry cheerfully asked, "Are we all met?"

Not familiar with Shakespeare, they all stared at him.

Seeing their confusion, Jerry soberly said, "Forget it..."

Meanwhile, Bill Connors had arrived at the courthouse early that morning and was surprised to find an unfamiliar horse and buggy tied to the hitching rail outside. After mounting the stairs to the second floor and gazing down the hallway, he was shocked to see Eugene Farnsworth slumped on the floor outside his office.

He ran over and quickly unlocked his office. Awkwardly dragging the old man in, he kicked the door shut and put him on the couch.   Seeing the blood-stained coat, Connors pulled it aside, lifted his shirt and saw that blood was coming through the tightly wound bandage. He brought over a glass of water and carefully sifted drops through the old man's parched lips.

Then he rose and looked down at the unconscious man. A thought came to him then and he walked over to the door, opened it quietly, and took a peek outside. No one was there yet. He sardonically noted that it was natural for Judge Alcott's courthouse to be the quietest building in the territory until the old crook had to put on a show of sentencing what he referred to as "rustlers". After shutting the door, the attorney returned to his "patient". He knew that Farnsworth had been either shot or stabbed and that he needed a doctor, not a prosecuting attorney. Yet the thought nagged at him: *In his suffering, why did he come crawling to him?*

Connors knew that this old reprobate was one of the Combine. He had met him a few times at the Cattlemen's House along with the other members of McDermott's group and sardonically recalled that he didn't like any of them. Without anyone ever telling him, he knew that if these ruthless men ever went down, he, as the city's chief prosecuting attorney holding his office while they perpetrated their crimes, would go down as well; and the Connors did not raise their son to be an idiot!

Still, he wondered what the old man wanted.

Fortunately, he had a Dutch oven in his office along with a standing pot of coffee in case he had to work late. Somehow, he would fix the old man up until he was awake enough to do some talking.

In another forty minutes, Farnsworth was sitting up on the couch, a mug of hot coffee in his hands.

"I'm here," he said, "because you're the only one in this town I can trust who'll listen to me."

Seated behind his desk, Connors looked at him oddly and repeated, "The only one you can trust? Listen, Farnsworth, I'm sure that hole in your side didn't take *that* much blood out of you. I'm Tad McDermott's city attorney, remember? I mean, how do you know I'm not going to tell Rawlins about your visit, or even ride over to Tad's ranch and tell him myself?"

Farnsworth looked at him with a sly smile over the rim of the steaming mug. Connors wryly noted the look and surmised that the close call with death seemed to have changed the old man.

"Because you're not as crooked as you let on," said Farnsworth. "Since my, shall we say 'resurrection', I've been able to sit back and remember little things that, as one of McDermott's lackeys, I never paid attention to before."

"Such as?"

"Such as the fact that when you tried the poor souls we referred to as rustlers, you kept recommending lower sentences. Damn it, man, only one of McDermott's toadies would fail to see that your heart wasn't in your work. You don't railroad honest men, Connors, that's just not your way."

Connors nodded thoughtfully but remained silent.

"Besides," Farnsworth said, grinning, "while I was being patched up by my kids, between bouts of semi-consciousness, I heard your name banded about as if you were an old friend."

Connors' eyes lowered to the clasped hands on his lap.

Farnsworth leaned forward and said, "It was *you* who told Morgan about the attempt to lynch Jill and Bingham."

Connors just looked at him, not answering.

Farnsworth's eyes crinkled at the corners and the smile he presented was warm and understanding. "Thank you, sir. You and Morgan saved my daughter's life." Then he looked away sadly. "I've been horrible to them. I'm not much of a father and not much of a man..."

Connors shifted in his chair, suddenly uncomfortable with the old man's sentiment.

"I'm not a father confessor," he said.

"No," Farnsworth said earnestly, "but if you get out pen and paper and write down everything I tell you, I promise that you'll have enough on McDermott and the rest to put an end to their operation once and for all."

"If that's the case," said Connors, "then you'd go down with them."

Farnsworth smiled again.

"I'm not afraid anymore..."

They begged for a 24-hour reprieve and, amazingly, they got it.

On the fourth-floor lounge of the Cattlemen's House, Tad McDermott's partners sat around him as he studied them through noxious cigar smoke and let them do all the talking. His eyes, however, betrayed the sheer hatred he had for them; as well as a persistent disgust with their cowardice.

Len Cagle was seated in another plush chair next to him, watching the look on his employer's face and understanding it completely. He also had no love for the three men seated around them. Wryly, he looked towards the chair that Farnsworth had always sat in and couldn't help smiling. He had no patience for traitors; while he rode with Quantrill, he had personally executed more than his share of them.

It was ten in the morning, and McDermott had ordered Charlie Quinn and his crew to hit the Carmody place and *then* attack the Cumberland ranch; a one-two punch instead of his grand ambition to attack them both simultaneously. Perhaps it was the good night's sleep (which he always had after a killing), or perhaps it was the bright, beautiful dawn that greeted him while his mount was brought down from the corral; but either way, McDermott's disposition seemed to be more understanding that morning.

"Don't worry," he reassured them flatly, "Charlie'll handle things today. But, tomorrow, gentlemen, I expect you to ride, and ride like demons."

Wilder, Ridgeway and Judge Alcott all nodded with relieved smiles and tried not to give each other any eye contact, as if they knew something Tad McDermott didn't. Indeed, they had met secretly after leaving his spread the previous night and they all decided to quit the Combine and quietly contact authorities in Omaha. They all had purchased train tickets to the state capital and were set to leave that night; this would put all of them safely out of the reach of Charlie Quinn and his killers. Then, once they arrived in the bustling metropolis, they were going to let the governor in on all of Tad McDermott's shenanigans, as well as those of Charlie Quinn and company. They would make themselves available to testify to their crimes, including the near-lynching of Jill Carmody and Jerry Bingham and the murders of dozens of homesteader families. Of course, their common pact was to ensure that they would never mention their own part in these dealings; the aim was to end Tad McDermott's domination of the valley—as well as their own domination by him—and allow them free rein to lord it over the homesteaders as they saw fit, though in a much quieter, if still illegal, way.

One thing was certain for all of them: They had witnessed true madness within the past three days when they saw two men who had been Tad McDermott's trusted allies gunned down before their eyes either by him or on his orders. They were frightened to death that one day soon, any one of them could be next.

"Thank you, Tad," said Judge Alcott.   "We'll be there tomorrow riding along with Charlie."

McDermott nodded absently. He didn't give a hoot whether these men approved of his decisions or not; he expected obedience, not phony gratitude.

Meanwhile, the servants in white coats and pressed trousers fluttered around them, offering drinks or little sweet cakes, but McDermott waved them away. The hired help at the Cattlemen's House knew that it was wise to look doubly subservient, and to keep their ears good and closed to the conversations of these ruthless men.

McDermott said, "We've put double guards on the corrals, in case the homesteaders make a play for our horse-flesh. I trust you gentlemen have done the same."

"Don't worry, Tad," said Ridgeway. "My hands at the Flying R are ready for trouble."

"Um-hm," said McDermott indifferently. He was loath to give any of his partners even the slightest bit of praise for their actions.

He said, "Right now, just sit back and we'll get news on Charlie's raid on the Carmody place, and then the Cumberland ranch. Catch those sons of bitches with their goddamn pants down a day before they raid *us*!"

He laughed shortly and noticed with annoyance that only Cagle was joining him. Shrugging it off, he ordered a brandy from a passing white-jacketed servant and tried not to linger on the fact that Bennett never returned from his mission to drop off Farnsworth's body in front of the Carmody ranch.

As he puffed on his cigar, his eyes narrowed thinking about it. Bennett may have been a loyal and stiff upper-lipped butler; but McDermott also knew that he liked a good whiskey and then a visit to Sadie's to sample one of the women. Something ate at him then, and he tried not to think that one of the women he had been "sampling" was the one who used to be his wife.

He shrugged again. In another hour or so, either Quinn or Hardy would personally report to him at the Cattlemen's House that Bingham and the Carmodys were finally in the ground where they belonged.

Charlie Quinn was riding south with his men, but during the ride, he suddenly decided to stop off at John Bright's place.

When Bright saw Quinn and his bunch through the window of his cabin, a shudder went through him. He quickly slung a rifle under his arm, careful to not make it look like he was pointing it at them, and reluctantly went outside to meet them at the fence.

Quinn leaned forward in the saddle and didn't waste any time with why they were there.

"Bright," he said plainly, "you're comin' with us."

The startled man looked at Quinn, and then at the other riders. Hardy saw the man's obvious fear and grinned.

"Me?" Bright asked. "Why me? If I ride with you, Cumberland's bunch will know I betrayed them."

"Well," said Quinn casually, "we realize that, John. But we're figurin' on makin' a clean sweep. So, who cares if a dead man thinks you betrayed him? Savvy? The boss gave those three overstuffed peacocks a reprieve and they ride with us tomorrow, but we could use an extra gun like you with us *today*. *Boss' orders, John.*"

Bright noticed that these last words were said coldly; there was no discussion on this point. Either he rode with them now, or he would die where he stood right then and there.

"Let me saddle a horse," he said weakly.

"Fine," said Quinn. "But don't take all day. Otherwise Al might have to follow you into the stable and speed you up some..."

Bright looked at Hardy's face and the wicked smile he saw chilled him.

They rode without haste in the direction of the Flying R.

As they headed north, Sam Cumberland made sure he was riding beside Morgan.

"Glad you're finally with us, Morgan."

"Thanks, Sam."

Cumberland paused for a moment, trying to find the right words.

"Haven't seen you at our place in a long time."

Morgan glanced at him, then faced the trail.

"That's because I've been somewhere no man should be, Sam."

"Yeah?" Cumberland asked curiously. "Where's that?"

"Buried within himself."

Cumberland nodded solemnly and said, "I see what you mean. You know, it takes a lot of ways to live. A man needs to be around people. Otherwise he becomes a…a recluse. He forgets there's others out there he owes something to."

Morgan glanced at him again. To Cumberland's surprise, he asked, "How's Sally?"

Cumberland suppressed his grin and asked, "You really want to know?"

Morgan said quietly, "Yeah, Sam, I really want to know."

"She misses you somethin' awful."

Morgan stared at the trail, a jumble of emotions rising within him.

"Uh-huh," he replied noncommittally.

"She was broken up when Emma Lou died, you know that."

"I know, Sam."

"And since then, she's given it almost a full year to keep her distance. Emma Lou was her best friend and she'll always respect her memory. But every time you dropped by, that is, when you got the chance, her eyes would light up when you entered a room. I watched her. I know. A father can sense these things."

Morgan paused again, his eyes straight ahead. Had this conversation happened a week earlier, Morgan would have scorned this attempt at matchmaking; but at that moment, he was angry no longer.

Morgan turned to look at him.

"You tell Sally that if I make it through this mess alive, I'd like to take her to the next barn dance in town...that is, if it's all right with you."

Cumberland grinned from ear to ear.

He put a huge hand on Morgan's shoulder and said, "You'll make it out alive if I have to strangle Charlie Quinn myself to make sure."

They rode at a leisurely pace through the valley's bottomlands, making sure they didn't kick up too much trail dust for anyone to see from a distance. Instead of riding at the head of the group, this time the two leaders had drifted back; they were confident of the men riding point and since they were not near anyone's property, they had no reason to expect trouble.

Al Hardy said, "Too bad we have to take the long way around."

Quinn replied, "That's why I'm keepin' the boys to a walk. No use kickin' up a cloud of dust they could see miles away. But the boss' orders were pretty plain. Now that Tad doesn't have Gene Farnsworth around anymore to tie his hands, our job is to wipe out the Carmodys and burn their place to the ground, no ifs, ands or buts."

Hardy's eyes lit up suddenly and he grinned slyly.

"Hey, Charlie. After we're doin' all that burnin' and killin', let's not kill that Carmody bitch right away."

Quinn glanced at him and said, "Oh? You have other ideas for her?"

"Just want her to have a little pleasure before she dies."

"Uh-huh. But she's kind of a wildcat, Al. She might not see it as pleasure."

"The hell with what she thinks. I figure I will!"

They both laughed then.

As the group headed further south, approaching one of the rows of foothills that were scattered throughout the valley, a harsh northerly wind suddenly blew dust in their faces...

Farnsworth was still holding the empty mug as he watched Connors, waiting for his reaction.

The attorney now had his coat and Stetson off. He had a notepad perched on his lap and he was finishing up the last of his writing. Then, putting his pen down and leaning back in his chair, he studied the old man before him.

"That's quite a story, Mister Farnsworth," he said. "Murder on an almost obscene scale, paying off crooked officials, theft that would make the worst highwayman look like an amateur. Mind you, I knew they were doing all these things, but even *I* didn't know it went this far. You should've taken this information to the governor months ago. A lot of folks might still be alive today if you had."

Despite the indictment, Farnsworth couldn't help smiling. Connors put it as plainly as he ever would; this was not the cagey lawyer talking now, this was the man himself. It only confirmed in his mind that bringing this information to Bill Connors had been the right thing to do.

Now he realized there was something else he had to do.

He suddenly dropped the mug to the floor and doubled over.

Connors bolted from his chair and ran over to the old man.

Wincing, Farnsworth looked up at him and said, "Doctor! Quick!"

The attorney nodded and grabbed his coat and Stetson.

"Hold on, Farnsworth," he said as he went out the door and closed it after him.

Donning his hat and coat as he went down the stairs, he knew that old Doc Griffin was two blocks away and figured to run all the way there. As he rushed down the street, past the looks of passersby wondering why the city attorney was in such a hurry, he was hoping he'd get back in time...

Farnsworth was watching from the office window as Connors disappeared around the corner, apparently headed for Doc Griffin's.

There was no better time than now.

With some difficulty he descended the stairs, then left the building and descended some more steps outside. Then he painfully climbed into the buggy, collapsed into the front seat and gigged the horse forward.

Taking deep breaths of the cool Nebraskan air, he sat back and calmly thought of what he would do once he got to the Cattlemen's House...

CHAPTER ELEVEN

As they rode in a northwesterly direction, something didn't feel right to Vladimir Jabotinsky. Riding point besides Sam Cumberland, he tried to listen to the sounds around the valley floor and the nearby foothills, but the trotting from the horses' hoofs made it hard.

He said urgently, "Sam, we should stop."

Cumberland looked at him and instantly raised his hand high. Obediently, the group behind them slowed down and then stopped.

Jerry and Jill glanced at each other and wondered what was going on. Not far from them, Morgan jacked a shell into his Winchester just in case.

Cumberland knew well enough to trust Jabotinsky's instincts. He was aware that the Russian, raised from the cradle to be alert to the sounds of a Cossack's horse, was prone to sense an enemy's approach more than most settlers. He had to; for his people, not being forewarned meant certain death.

Jabotinsky cocked an ear for a moment; then he stared at the horses.

His voice was no louder than a harsh whisper.

"Sam, look at the horses."

Cumberland looked at his own, and then the others around him. The mounts were tense, their ears pricking up as they sensed the approach of others.

He and Jabotinsky eyed each other and both silently agreed that other horses were approaching at a walk very close nearby.

Without a word, they both slid their rifles from their scabbards. When Cumberland turned around and scanned the group behind them, the others read his look and also unsheathed their rifles. Then, putting his finger to his lips for quiet, he gestured for them to be ready to ride forward and start shooting.

Coming slowly around the bend, Hardy looked at his mount and couldn't help noticing the change in him.

"What the hell the matter with him?" he asked no one in particular.

Quinn glanced at him and said, "What?"

As their group continued circling the foot of the hill, Hardy said, "Damn animal's actin' like a pack of lions is around that bend."

Quinn sat bolt upright in his saddle and stared at the horses. He knew exactly what their fidgeting meant.

"Jesus Christ!" he exclaimed as he yanked on the reins.

But it was too late. The crew had turned the bend and now found themselves face to face with Cumberland's group with nothing more than fifty yards between them.

McDermott's men had just seconds to see their enemies. They were no longer attacking helpless families with children in tow, and their reactions to these new enemies were not those of fighting men at all. They fumbled for their rifles, their horror at seeing their enemies right before them caused some of them to free their Winchesters from their scabbards, but sweaty fingers nervously dropped them to the ground. These men were then forced to waste precious seconds dismounting and then bending over to pick up their weapons. Some of them stayed in the saddle and, as second nature, drew their pistols instead.

Cumberland's group, however, wasted no time.

As one, they opened fire on McDermott's crew and cut most of them down, many of their victims plunging off saddles and falling heavily to the ground amidst clouds of gun smoke as the air filled with the stench of ignited sulfur and the rancid sweat of crazed horses, suddenly wheeling around to avoid the enemy's fire. Some of McDermott's crew still had their feet clinging to stirrups and the gunfire so frightened the horses that their riders were dragged all over the valley floor, their bodies bouncing painfully and finally over the many jutting rocks along the ground. The men who had given their victims no chance, were now getting slaughtered as they frantically reached for weapons they did not have a chance to use.

In the spilt second before the shooting commenced, Quinn and Hardy, safely in the rear, had turned their horses west and sped off, away from their beaten comrades. They rode like demons across the flat terrain and in short order put miles between themselves and Cumberland's group. Seeing their own leaders fleeing the scene of battle now that the odds weren't in their favor, two riders broke from the pack and also sped off, following Quinn and Hardy at a fast clip.

At that point, the old Texan, Curtis Rogers, lifted his rifle to his shoulder and fired. The first man's arms raised high in the air and he spilled from his horse. Then Rogers sighted along the barrel at the other figure and fired. The second man's body jolted forward, somersaulted over his horse's head and hit the ground. The two mounts, now rider-less, kept running on into the open country until they finally slowed down and drifted along several miles away.

Caught in the middle of the shootout, John Bright tried to raise himself in the stirrups and shout to the group that he was one of them, but a rifle cartridge hit him dead in the throat and he toppled from his horse to the ground.

Jerry, his rifle still smoking, cursed and watched in frustration as Quinn and Hardy rode off through the valley.

Then a cry besides him caused him to turn and see Jill toppling from her horse. He dropped his rifle to the ground and grabbed her before she fell off.

"Jill! Jill!" He shook her and her Stetson fell off as he held her. Looking her over, he quickly saw the blood form through the left elbow of her buckskin jacket. He pulled the smoking rifle out of her clinging right hand and tossed it aside. Then he dismounted and gently pulled her off her horse.

He carried her over to a shaded spot at the bottom of the hill and gently set her down. She winced painfully when her arm touched the gravel on the hillside.

In seconds, it was all over. Most of the homesteaders dismounted and walked over to the dead McDermott riders that littered the ground around the foot of the hill, rifles at the ready. However, they saw very quickly that their weapons were not needed.

Jabotinsky looked at the bodies and said wryly, "I wish they were Cossacks."

"Clean sweep," said Cumberland.

"Not quite. Two of 'em got away."

Jerry heard him and said earnestly, "Not yet they haven't!"

Then, in a speed that surprised the others, that is, for an easterner, Jerry quickly mounted his horse. Unfortunately, when he threw his leg over the horse's back, the pistol Jerry wore on his hip tumbled out of the holster.

Looking down at Cumberland and Jabotinsky, he said, "Take care of her!" Then he gave a kick to the horse's flank and sped off across the valley in the same direction that Quinn and Hardy had taken.

Jabotinsky asked, "Now what is that crazy man going to do all by himself?"

Cumberland replied, "He's got a score to settle. When that happens, you don't think of the odds against you..."

From the hillside, Jill cried out, "Morgan!"

Her brother had not dismounted and presently he rode over and gazed down at Jill. He quickly saw the worry in her pale face and understood.

Brandishing his still-smoking Winchester, he smiled gravely and said, "Don't worry, big sister. I won't let anything happen to him..."

Then with a yell, he turned his horse and spurred him in the direction of the others.

Cumberland shouted after him, "Be careful, son!"

He and Jabotinsky watched as Morgan and his horse got smaller and smaller and finally disappeared in the distance.

Hank came up to them holding his rifle. The young man was smiling from ear to ear.

"We were lucky, gents!" he said excitedly. "Some of us got hit, but from what I see, none of the wounds are what you would call 'lethal'. We surprised the hell out of 'em! All in all, I'd say the danger is over."

Jabotinsky just stared in the direction that the others took and said quietly, "That's what you think."

Eugene Farnsworth steered the buggy up to the boardwalk just a block away from the front of the Cattlemen's House and then climbed out. His coat pockets were stuffed with the items he had stolen from Morgan's tool shed. He got a little dizzy as his feet touched the ground and he held on to the edge of the buggy seat to steady himself. Gratefully, he inhaled a good lungful of cool air and tried not to appear as if he needed any help. Someone passing by and seeing him ill would stop and make him the center of attention; at this point in his plans, he realized that stealth and secrecy were all-important. He saw no reason to reveal his return from the dead so close to the seat of Tad McDermott's kingdom.

Farnsworth hobbled awkwardly down the boardwalk, trying to avert eye contact with anyone passing by in the opposite direction. However, he still received some stares; not walking straight was something he couldn't help since his wound had not healed properly, but all that was beyond his concern now.

Soon, he found himself in front of the Cattlemen's House and staring up at its four floors; it was the tallest building in town. How many dirty deals had he been privy to and profited by; how many murders had he planned along with the others? That would all end now.

Seeing him, a doorman opened the huge gated front door for him, and he stepped aside.

Not seeing anything wrong, the doorman greeted him pleasantly.

"Good morning, Mister Farnsworth."

"Good morning, John," he replied, straining to put some cheer into his voice.

Farnsworth was grateful that Connors had given him an extra coat to replace the bloody one he had before. The doorman would *really* stare at him had he worn that!

Carefully, Farnsworth walked across the sprawling lobby, its plush red carpeting soft beneath his boots. Suddenly, he felt something wet running down his leg. Trying not to appear as if something was wrong, he casually opened his coat and his eyes peered down at his right side. He instantly saw that blood had not only spread throughout the bandage again, but that it was also dripping down to the ground. Looking down, he saw the red splotches form in the rug. Silently, he thanked God that the rug was the same color, if not the same shade, as his blood. The stains were something others would not have noticed unless one was actually looking for blood; and that was *not* one of the various duties of the employees of the Cattlemen's House.

For Eugene Farnsworth, it was too late to back out now.

He quietly entered the open elevator. The young man who stood at the switch smiled and greeted him.

"Morning, Mister Farnsworth."

"Morning, Kenneth." Farnsworth tried to sound cheerful but couldn't keep the weariness out of his voice.

Kenneth glanced at him oddly for a moment, then pulled slightly on the door handle. The steel door then slid closed with a hiss.

"You're just in time, sir."

Farnsworth looked at him curiously.

Seeing the look, Kenneth explained, "Mister McDermott and your other partners are still in the study. They haven't left yet."

"Ahh!" said Farnsworth, with a grin. "Well, Kenneth, I'll get off on three right now."

Kenneth looked at him strangely.

Farnsworth explained, "I just want to see Cremins."

Pete Cremins was the building manager whose office was on the third floor. Kenneth nodded as if understanding and threw the switch forward. In a moment, the elevator lurched upwards and Farnsworth looked at the young man with some irritation. *What business was it of his where he was going anyway?*

He figured to get off on the third floor and then walk up the stairway to the fourth. He had no intention of running into his former partners as the elevator door opened and then find himself trapped, especially by Tad McDermott; he knew that they wouldn't walk down so he would retain the element of surprise by coming up the stairs.

Bill Connors threw open the door to his office and entered, with Doc Griffin carrying his black bag close behind him. Shocked to see the office empty, Connors went across the room and looked out the window.

"Okay, Bill," said the doc. "Where is he? He didn't jump out the window, did he? I think we would've seen that."

Connors pulled his head back inside and walked around his desk. Then, in a rare display of fury, he cursed and threw his fist against the plastered wall, putting a sizable dent in it. Griffin stared at him, clearly not familiar with the sight of Bill Connors losing his temper so demonstratively.

"Take it easy, Bill."

Connors repeated angrily, "'Take it easy!'" Then he calmed down enough for him to explain his rage. "Doc, I've just been suckered worse than any rube in a crooked card game. Me! Conned into leaving that old man alone for five minutes and he runs out before I get back, pretending he's more hurt than he was. He was a good actor and I was a gullible audience and I fell for it!"

Griffin said gently, "Bill, don't blame yourself. If he's as hurt as you say, he couldn't have gone far."

Then Connors stared at the doc with a sudden realization.

He said urgently, "That horse and buggy that was in front. It's not there now!"

"Horse and buggy?"

"He drove it here." Connors then moved quickly across the

room and went to his closet. He threw open the door, reached inside and pulled out his Winchester.

The doc was startled. He asked, "What're you gonna do with that?"

Connors checked the loads and said, "I think I know where he went. And he's going to need some help..."

Marshal Rawlins stood in front of his office and idly watched the street. He knew about the attack on the Carmody place and, as instructed by Tad McDermott, was fully prepared to refer to the raid as a preemptive strike against the rustling element. So, when the sound of galloping horses came from the end of the street, he figured that the boys had finished their job.

Then he noticed something strange.

As a mother and her little girl were crossing the street, the two riders barreling into town didn't stop. The horses were galloping in at top speed and the young mother screamed and grabbed her daughter as they came near. The now-lathered animals, spurred beyond endurance, came within inches of trampling the little girl, but her quick-acting mother yanked her back so hard that they toppled backwards onto the boardwalk from which they had just stepped off. The two were shaken, but not hurt.

Witnessing the scene from down the street, a rage went through Rawlins. No one was going to get away with something like that in *his* town.

He then stepped out into the street and yelled at the riders to stop. Seeing that they were still speeding towards him, he started to pull his gun, but before he could complete the draw, they were upon him. Screaming, Rawlins went down under the hooves of the first horse and was then further trampled into the earth by the second.

The passersby on the boardwalks watched the sight in horror; at least two women fainted.

Not stopping for a moment, the two riders kept going and then turned left at the end of the street, still maintaining their frantic pace.

Behind them, the late Marshal Rawlins lay in a pool of his own blood...

As they slowed their horses down and then stopped in front of the Cattlemen's House, Hardy said, "Damn phony law dog, gettin' in our way..."

They dismounted and tied their mounts to the hitching rail in front.

"Hell with 'em," said Quinn. "I've got a peck of money comin' to me, and the boss man better be ready to pay off."

As the doorman automatically opened the door for them, he looked at them oddly, but then remembered them as men who rode for Tad McDermott. Ignoring him, Quinn and Hardy went through the lobby and headed for the elevator.

Hardy pushed on the button impatiently.

"Wonder if we shouldn't take the stairs," he said.

Quinn looked up at the arrow above the elevator door and said, "It'll get us there quicker than if we climbed four flights of stairs. I just want to get my money and head to Mexico before them homesteaders get wise to where we are."

Hardy said, "Now that you mention it, I could've sworn I heard a lone horse followin' us."

"Yeah, well, if he gets too close, it'll be too bad for him."

Hardy impatiently punched the elevator button again.

"Come on, you damn new-fangled contraption!"

"Hell with it," Quinn said. "Let's take the stairs. Damn thing probably got some mechanical problem. Shows what happens when they trust these machines they bring from the east..."

However, Kenneth couldn't go back to the first floor yet despite the constant buzzing sound from the elevator's wall panel.

"Jesus," the young man said irritably, "I'll be back down in a minute!"

He had already dropped off Farnsworth on the third floor but didn't know that the old man was already climbing up the last flight of stairs to the fourth.

Meanwhile, Honus Wilder, Pete Ridgeway and Judge Alcott were all getting up from their chairs and making apologies to Tad McDermott.

"Where are all of you going?" he demanded to know.

Ridgeway said, "We just wanted to get some breakfast at Kate's. We'll be right back."

"That's right, Tad," said Wilder, trying to sound pleasant. "We'll return in a few minutes."

McDermott eyed them suspiciously and said, "Francois could cook up anything you boys wanted. What do you want to go to a flea-pit coffee house like Kate's for?"

The three men were shrugging into their long coats and putting on their hats. They tried not to give each other eye contact, but to McDermott it was plain that something wasn't quite right.

In reality the three men had talked at length just before this morning's meeting and were well aware that McDermott planned a final raid on the Carmody and the Cumberland spreads. They had decided that, if and when Quinn reported the results of his raid personally to McDermott, they, the three remaining members of the Combine, would not be there when it happened. For they realized all too well that, to the staff and servants at the Cattle-men's House, the very presence of the three men in proximity to McDermott and Quinn would imply that they themselves were part of a murderous conspiracy. They knew that employees of the Cattlemen's House might be called as witnesses after they reported all they knew to the authorities in Omaha, and they were getting as far away from McDermott as they possibly could. Their bags were already packed for the long ride to Omaha that night.

Anxiously, the three men were hoping that this would be the last time they'd ever see Tad McDermott; as it turned out, they were right.

Before their boss could make another protest, the three men quickly headed out the open doorway. McDermott and Len Cagle eyed each other, not liking this at all.

McDermott said quietly, "Follow 'em, Len. I've got a feelin' those three snakes are up to something."

With a silent nod, Cagle grabbed his coat and Stetson and put them on as he went out the door.

The elevator was only forty feet away at the end of the hall.

Wilder nervously asked, "Think he suspects something?"

"No," said Ridgeway. "He's just normally suspicious."

Mopping his brow with a handkerchief, Judge Alcott said, "Gentlemen, the sooner we get out of here, the better."

As they passed the stairway, they were so absorbed in their own dilemmas that they didn't notice the figure of a man in a long black coat coming up the stairs.

After they arrived at the elevator, which was just a dozen feet past the top of the stairs, Judge Alcott nervously punched the button on the wall near him.

They practically jumped when Cagle appeared behind them and said, "Gentlemen, mind if I join you?" It was not a friendly question; it was a command. He was joining them whether they liked it or not.

The three men before him were openly scared now; they knew that if McDermott sent Cagle out to join them, that he was definitely suspicious. They tried to hide the fear in their sweaty faces.

As Farnsworth climbed the last flight of stairs and neared the top, he heard the voices of his three ex-partners, as well Len Cagle's.

He was seething inside.

Weakly, he finally got to the top of the stairs and stood on the fourth floor, watching them as they waited for the elevator, their backs to him.

Reaching into his coat pocket, he removed a stick of dynamite and, with a thumbnail, struck a match alight. Then he put the burning match to the fuse and walked towards them.

It was not only the harsh odor of the burning fuse that alerted them, but the hissing sound as well. The four men turned around to face him, suddenly horrified at the sight of a man who was supposed to be dead.

Ridgeway said, "Jesus Christ, Farnsworth!"

Wilder gasped and grasped his chest, though he wasn't getting a heart attack.

Judge Alcott shouted, "Are you crazy, man! That's dynamite!"

Cagle said nothing, for what good would it do? Also, displaying fear was just not his way.

Quietly, Farnsworth kept approaching them, holding the burning stick of dynamite before him.

With a surprisingly strong voice, he said angrily, "You laughed at my daughter when McDermott kicked her while she was lying on the ground! And then you laughed at *me* when that bastard had one of his killers shoot me! Well, why aren't you laughing now?"

Just then, the elevator arrived, and Kenneth pulled the door open.

The young man started to say, "All right, gentlemen, we're headed down—"

But he didn't finish the sentence.

Cagle suddenly reached into the elevator, grabbed the young man by the lapels of his uniform coat and pulled him out. Kenneth was so surprised by the attack that he was helpless to stop himself from flying towards the wall right of the elevator. He suddenly struck his head against it and dropped to the ground, unconscious.

The four men quickly piled into the elevator and Ridgeway, the last man in, pulled on the door. With an audible hiss, the door started to slide closed.

Then, just before it closed completely, Farnsworth tossed the stick of dynamite into the elevator. In that split second, he delighted in hearing his three ex-partners scream in terror just before the door closed. Cagle tried to draw his gun, but the three frightened men blocked his view of Farnsworth before the door slid shut. The closed elevator door was the last thing he would ever see.

A terrific explosion blew the elevator apart and shook the building to its foundations. The door burst out into the hallway and flew several yards down the corridor, past Farnsworth, who flattened himself against the left wall, and it finally landed a few yards beyond the study. Inside the shaft, the elevator cables snapped completely. Then the elevator floor broke off and hurtled down the shaft to the basement far below. Inside the burnt wreckage of what had once been an elevator, the four bodies of Len Cagle, Honus Wilder, Pete Ridgeway and Judge Alcott, now charred black, followed the floor panel and dropped heavily down the shaft to the bottom. Only the small ceiling of the elevator remained attached to the broken cables. After a few seconds, it too snapped and plunged towards the basement; the crash echoed through the building.

Farnsworth collapsed against the wall and slid to the floor. That particular action had taken a lot out of him. Down the hall, servants were running around in panic. Huge clouds of thick, black smoke drifted up from the open shaft and were filling the fourth-floor hallway.

Tad McDermott had been seated where he was, stewing over why his partners were abruptly going out for breakfast instead of awaiting news of Quinn's victory, when he heard the explosion. The floor trembled beneath him and he shot up from his chair and headed for the door. Angrily, he shoved running servants out of his way and, after he got to the open doorway, stared at the carnage down the hall.

The smoke was thick, and as he stared at the sight, he could barely make out a large hole where the elevator door used to be. So focused was he on the sight that he didn't notice the crumpled figure of a dying man on the floor to the right, or the young man with the blood on his scalp rising off the ground on the left.

Kenneth's forehead was bleeding, and as he rose dizzily, he tried to keep himself from falling. He saw what had happened and his eyes were tearing up from the thick smoke around him; he knew he *had* to get out of there.

Stumbling away from the epicenter of the blast, Kenneth reached the top of the stairs and started to join the crowd of servants madly descending them when McDermott grabbed his arm and yanked him around.

"What the hell is goin' on!" he shouted above the noise.

However, Kenneth was no longer the polite elevator man who

bowed to his passengers. Angrily, he pulled his arm away and yelled, "Get away from me, you bastard!"

Undeterred, McDermott again grabbed his arm in his iron grip and pulled him around to face him. Then he drew one of his .45s and put it to the young man's head.

"Listen, you little whelp," he shouted, "you tell me what happened, or I'll blow your goddamn brains out right now!"

The young man's eyes lost their defiance and he shrank under the cold, metallic touch of the pistol barrel against his bleeding skull.

"Honest, Mister McDermott," he said, "I was coming up in the elevator and picking up your partners when Mister Cagle threw me against the wall. I don't know what happened next. The whole elevator must've blown up with them still inside!"

McDermott stared at the young man, his eyes scanning the stairs behind him. The last of the cooks and servants had fled down the stairs and suddenly, they were all alone.

"What happened?" Kenneth asked, his defiance returning. "Did someone get back at your partners for one of your dirty deals?"

The remark, sounding so blunt and bitter coming from a young man who had once been no more than a servant, suddenly angered McDermott; it not only proved that the employees of the Cattlemen's House knew what the Combine was doing, but (and this is what *really* angered him) they were being deferential, while in reality hating their guts.

McDermott didn't even think twice; he lowered the gun to Kenneth's chest and fired. The young man's eyes bulged in surprise and shock. Then he tumbled back down the flight of stairs behind him, finally stopping, upside down, just before the last step above the third-floor landing, his blood soaking the plush red carpet.

McDermott eyed him for about two seconds, then holstered his gun and turned back towards the study. Moving quickly through the empty room, he went to the window and lifted it all the way up. Then he proceeded to climb down the building's fire escape.

Jerry rode hard into town. He was close enough to see Quinn and Hardy ride down Palmer Street and then turn their mounts fast into Third. As he sped down Palmer, he immediately saw the crowd gathered in the middle of the street and slowed down to a walk.

He stopped in front of the crowd and several townspeople looked up at him.

"What happened?" he asked a sodbuster standing near him.

The farmer looked up and said, "Charlie Quinn and Al Hardy just ran down the marshal."

Jerry peered through gaps in the crowd and glimpsed a bloodied body lying in the road. He immediately winced at the sight.

The sodbuster, an old man in dirty overalls, smiled crookedly and said, "Ain't a pretty sight, is it?"

"No, it isn't," Jerry replied. "But Quinn and Hardy turned their horses down Third Street. What's down that way?"

The farmer rubbed his sizable brown beard and said, "Nothin' I recollect worth goin' to, 'cept the Cattlemen's House—"

Before the old man finished his sentence, Jerry put his heels to the horse and went around the crowd. He rode to the end of the street and then made a left turn down Third at a fast clip...

CHAPTER TWELVE

QUINN AND HARDY HAD JUST SET FOOT ON THE SECOND FLOOR when the explosion shook the building. They were knocked off their feet and fell opposite the stairway railing. After a few moments, the upstairs servants and other workers came down from the upper floors. Stunned by the impact of the blast, the two men were still shaking their heads and rising off the ground when the servants piled down the stairs, went right past them and continued their descent.

After they got up, they gave each other knowing glances.

Hardy asked, "You think someone tried to kill the boss?"

Quinn said, "That's what I aim to find out. I don't want that man dead until he pays us off..."

Suddenly, they heard the gunshot and both men flattened themselves against the wall and drew their guns.

Hardy said, "What the hell!"

Quinn said tightly, "*Somethin's* goin' on up there! Come on!"

With their guns before them, they started to ascend the stairs.

Jerry was just in time to see the fourth floor at the east side of the building blow out into the street.

His horse reared back violently as piles of wood and mortar rained down onto the street. Jerry quickly pulled his feet out of the stirrups and dropped to the ground before his mount threw him off. With his hands before him, he was able to break his fall and roll away from the crazed horse's descending hooves before they stomped him. He ignored his fallen derby hat and from the ground watched as his horse fled down the street in terror.

Jerry suddenly realized that he had dropped his rifle back at the gunfight ocation. When he looked down at his holster, he was shocked to see that it was empty.

This was just *not* his day.

Looking up at the huge smoking hole in the building's east wall, Jerry didn't know what was going on, but he had to find out, gun or no gun. He rose from the ground and, hearing the approaching noise, moved out of the way just in time as the employees of the Cattlemen's House burst out the front door and ran past him in all directions.

After the last man cleared the doorway, he ducked inside as the door was still open, and moved quickly through the lobby. As he passed the closed elevator shaft on the ground floor, he noticed the thick and noxious smoke billowing out through the outer door and guessed that whatever happened, it had originated there.

Then he mounted the stairs.

Unlike either Jerry, who stopped to ask the crowd what was happening, or Quinn and Hardy, who murderously rode through anyone who happened to be in their way, Morgan shot down the street, howling at the top of his lungs.

The crowd that had gathered in the street quickly got the message. They scattered in all directions as his mount barreled through. Morgan was still howling as he disappeared down the street and then turned fast into Third.

As his horse went past the courthouse building, Bill Connors heard the yell and had just enough time to jump back onto the boardwalk. Doc Griffin caught him just before he fell to the ground.

Gazing down the street after the speeding horse and rider, Connors exclaimed, "Morgan!" He had not seen Jerry ride by since the New Yorker had ridden past the courthouse before the attorney had left it.

Holding onto Connors' arm, Griffin said, "That man almost killed you!"

"Nonsense," said Connors, pulling his arm away. "What do you think he was yelling like that for? Obviously, to warn passersby to get the hell out of the way. It figures. He's also headed for the Cattlemen's House."

"Also?"

"Just be nearby, Doc. I think we're going to need you..."

Then they heard the explosion.

"Holy Jesus!" Griffin exclaimed.

Connors said, "See what I mean?"

Quinn and Hardy climbed up past the third floor and then stopped in their tracks when they saw Kenneth's dead body sprawled on the steps. They exchanged looks. Then they gingerly stepped over the young man's body and climbed up to the fourth floor.

The smoke coming from the open elevator shaft was thick, and they coughed as they looked around the corridor.

Quinn saw the doorway to the study and said, "Stay here. I'll see if the boss is there."

Holding his gun before him, he carefully stepped inside the room.

Jerry had just gotten to the third floor and was turning to the next flight of steps when he suddenly saw Kenneth's body and gasped.

The noise alerted Hardy, who was standing at the top of the stairs. After spotting the figure on the staircase, he quickly ducked behind the wall. Then he quietly cocked the hammer of his pistol and waited.

However, with black smoke all around him, he didn't see the battered old man on the floor just a few feet behind him.

When Jerry finally set foot on the fourth floor, Farnsworth screamed, "Bingham!"

The sound so startled Hardy that his shot went wild.

In the smoky din of the corridor, Jerry could still see Hardy turn the gun towards him, but before he could fire again, the New Yorker grabbed his arm and pushed it up. Another shot was fired, and a bullet drilled into the ornate ceiling.

Angrily, Jerry yanked the wrist back all the way until the gunman cried out in pain. In seconds, the gun fell to the floor. Then Jerry punched the gunman hard in the face and saw him fall back on the carpeted floor. With a rage coursing through him, he jumped on the prone man and the two ended up rolling all over the floor, bunching up the torn carpet and dangerously getting close to the open shaft.

Farnsworth flattened himself against the wall in an effort to avoid the tussling men. Then, the sound of running feet could be heard from the study and Quinn appeared in the doorway. He saw the fight down the hall and aimed his gun at the two men, patiently waiting for the right moment. It wasn't long in coming.

Jerry rolled on top of Hardy and kept hitting the man until his knuckles bled.

Now with Jerry's broad back in his sights, Quinn cocked the hammer of his pistol.

Then, from somewhere below him, he suddenly heard, "Quinn!"

He turned to the sound and saw Morgan on the third-floor staircase, bringing his rifle up to his shoulder. Quinn quickly aimed his pistol, trying to see his enemy through the remaining smoke that hovered in the air.

As Morgan spotted him in his sights, tears started to form, and not just from the smoke. He was thinking of Emmy Lou and how she had been taken away from him all too soon.

But tears or no tears, he saw Quinn as clearly as he did that tree branch that day when he shot it apart and rescued his sister and Jerry Bingham from a lynching.

Quinn fired, but the smoke that still hung in the air obscured his vision, and his shot ricocheted off the banister. Then, before the gunman could get a clearer shot, Morgan fired and the bullet hit Charlie Quinn square in the forehead, effectively blowing away the back of his skull. The near-headless body dropped the pistol and fell completely over the fourth-floor railing. Morgan watched its rapid descent until it hit the first floor in a splatter of blood and tissue.

Hearing the shots, fear took hold of Hardy and he found the renewed strength to push his tormentor off him. He was now hatless, and his puffed-up face was bleeding from the nose and mouth. Caught off guard, Jerry fell back on the floor just as Hardy leapt to his feet. But the gunman could not gain his footing; his booted feet were now tangled in the bunched-up hallway rug and, trying to free himself, he fell back into the open shaft.

Reaching out as he fell, Hardy grabbed hold of one of the severed cables and his feet swung out over the void. Suddenly, the gunman felt an intense shock and his face contorted in pain as free-running electricity, still active within the severed cable, coursed throughout his body.

Pushing himself off the floor, Jerry watched in horror as Hardy writhed to and fro, his hands forced to cling to the live cable as his face twisted in fear and pain.

Then, suddenly it was over. The now-overheated cable burst forth in an explosion of fire and sparks and Hardy, whose hands were burnt to a crisp, now had nothing to hold him aloft anymore. He plummeted down the shaft, his screams of agony echoing up to the fourth floor. Jerry gazed down the shaft, a chill running through him as he did so.

Morgan had arrived just in time to see the gunman fall.

"Jesus, Bingham," he said drily, "you play rough."

The slight movement on the floor behind them made them both turn and see Farnsworth trying to sit up against the wall.

Gazing up at Morgan, the old man said, "You beat 'em! Didn't you, son?"

Morgan stared down at the crumpled figure and instantly realized what his stepfather had done. Tears came to his eyes again.

Choking up, he said, "We *all* beat 'em, Dad..."

Farnsworth smiled weakly. Then he closed his eyes. It was the last thing he ever did.

It took a while, seeing that he wasn't a young man anymore, but McDermott finally made it to the bottom of the fire-escape stairs, then got on the bottom ladder and rode it to the ground. After he leapt off it, the ladder sprang back up and he looked around irritably. He found himself in the alleyway between the Cattlemen's House and the bank.

Quickly, he moved forward towards the street. However, when he emerged from the alley, he was met by a crowd of men consisting of Cumberland's crew and many of the townsmen, this group led by Connors. All of them were pointing rifles, shotguns and pistols at the last surviving member of the Combine.

With a sneer, McDermott said, "So this is where it's gonna end, eh?"

Connors said, "The killing's got to stop, Tad, and this is as good a place as any to stop it."

McDermott's eyes narrowed into slits and he snarled, "I bought you, Connors. I bought all of you! This whole town and all the lives in it! Lock, stock and barrel!"

Cumberland said, "We're not your property, McDermott. We're people! Your trouble is you forgot that long ago."

McDermott continued to stare back at them, the hatred plain in his hard face.

"Enough of this stupid jawin'!" he finally shouted. "Let's dance!"

Then he pulled both of his pistols from his twin shoulder holsters in a fast cross-draw. Pointing the big guns at the crowd, he fired both of them rapidly, trying to gun down as many of his enemies as possible.

He was a good shot; Pete Hamlin fell with a bullet in the stomach and Connors received a wound in the left shoulder blade. Several townsmen were also hit in the melee.

Then the crowd returned fire with everything they had.

Tad McDermott was riddled by dozens of bullets, rifle cartridges and shotgun shells. His body, now a bloody mess, was still standing for another few seconds before the arms that held the guns lowered and the once tall and proud figure toppled backwards into a mud puddle at the mouth of the alley.

Connors lowered his rifle and stepped forward. Holding his bloody shoulder with his free hand, he looked down at the body of Tad McDermott.

He said, "I wish I could say some quote that would fit the occasion of this man's death."

Jabotinsky, looking down at the body, said contemptuously, "He should burn in hell!" However, he said this in Hebrew.

Connors said, "I don't know what that means, but I guess it's appropriate."

Jerry and Morgan left the building and walked over to the crowd.

Morgan approached Cumberland and said, "Quinn and Hardy won't be bothering us anymore."

The big homesteader smiled and put his hand on the young man's shoulder. Then he pulled him aside to talk to him.

It was another ten minutes before Jill and Hank Austin came up the street on their horses. Jill's left arm had a tourniquet tied to it above her wounded elbow, and Hank was holding her horse's reins and pulling it behind him. Then the young man dismounted and helped Jill down from her horse. When she turned and saw Jerry, she ran towards him and threw her right arm around his neck, embracing him tightly.

He said excitedly, "We got 'em, Jill. All of 'em. We got our land back."

Jill pulled back and looked at him oddly.

She said, "*Our* land?"

Awkwardly, Jerry was about to explain until they heard Connors, standing nearby, clear his throat.

"Excuse me," he said apologetically, "couldn't help overhearing." He looked at Jerry and said, "You know, Bingham, I could use a man in my office who's not afraid to get the job done."

Jerry replied, "I don't know, Connors. I'm a New Yorker and the roots are kind of deep."

The attorney looked at him levelly and said, "You've got one hundred sixty acres coming to you from your father's land. And after I furnish the governor with the information that Jill's father gave me, big changes will be in order. The state might be carving up all of McDermott's land and those of the Combine to give to the homesteaders—and if you stick around and work for me, that might include *you*, my friend. So, think about it. Right now, I've got an urgent appointment with Doc Griffin." He raised his good arm and tipped his hat to Jill, then started to walk away.

"Besides," he added, "everyone knows that New York is riddled with crime."

After he left, Jerry looked into Jill's eyes and asked, "Well, can you think of another reason for me to stay here?"

Jill smiled and nodded.

"Uh-huh," he said. "That day when Morgan was driving us in the buggy after our near-lynching when you were beside me in the seat and snuggling your head into my chest, you weren't sleeping, were you?"

"No, I wasn't."

"And when Morgan said that a good man should take you away from all this, you heard it?"

Grinning, she nodded.

Jerry looked thoughtful for a moment. Then he said, "Well, New York is kinda crime-ridden…"

Tightening her hold on his neck, Jill said, "In that case, Mister Bingham, what you need is a *good woman* to take you away from all that." Then she pulled him close and they kissed long and hard in the middle of Third Street.

Meanwhile, over by McDermott's body, a shabby looking dog wandered over to it and quietly marked his own territory…

IF YOU LIKED THIS BOOK
YOU MIGHT LIKE: THE
DERBY MAN: OMNIBUS

BY GARY MCCARTHY

**FROM SPUR AWARD WINNER GARY MCCARTHY
COMES AN UNLIKELY HERO IN THE DERBY MAN
SERIES...**

Darby Buckingham was an unlikely candidate for western frontier
life. From his round-toed shoes to his derby hat, he was a man of
culture, a creature of comfort, who liked his gourmet restaurants
and expensive cigars.

The short, stocky New Yorker made a fortune writing dime
novels about the old west. Now he was out west to do some
research for his next novel, little suspecting that he would be
learning firsthand about frontier justice and frontier heroism.

**Darby Buckingham quickly became the West's
hardest hitting, toughest fighting, fastest thinking
hero!**

AVAILABLE NOW

ABOUT THE AUTHOR

BOB HERZBERG was born in Brooklyn, N.Y. in 1956. He had graduated from Erasmus Hall High School and went on to take a variety of jobs, from truck driver to warehouse manager to salesman. He always wanted to act in plays and do comedy and soon started performing in community theaters and colleges around New York. By the 1990s, Bob had performed standup comedy, improv and murder mystery/dinner theater at clubs in both N.Y. and Hollywood. Around the same time, he wrote and co-starred in *The Melnicks* series on local TV, which had been aired on both coasts. In 2006, he started writing western novels and mysteries. He is a member of Western Writers of America, International Thriller Writers and the Dramatists' Guild. In the past six years he has had four books published: *Shooting Scripts, From Pulp Western to Film*, which is about western authors and the films made from their works; *The FBI & the Movies*, which focuses on films with FBI characters and the Bureau's influence on these productions; *Savages & Saints: the Changing Image of American Indian in Westerns*, which details the Indian Wars and the films made about them; and *The Left Side of the Screen* which focuses on Communists and Liberals in Hollywood during the years 1929-2009. In 2008, he appeared on TV-Land's *Myths & Scandals* in a sequence about the FBI; in 2013, he appeared as a commentator on the 20th anniversary Blu-ray edition of *The Fugitive*. Bob latest, *Revolutionary Mexico on Film, 1914-2014*, will be released in 2015. He's been happily married to the lovely actress/poet Colleen Hayden. One day they hope to live out west.